Shortly [illegible] nes published in *The* [illegible] accomplished and best-known [illegible] century, M. R. James. At the same time *The* [illegible] a competition offering prizes of £500 and £200 for [illegible] best original, previously unpublished ghost stories. The judges were Kingsley Amis, whose ghost story *The Green Man* became one of his most widely praised novels; Patricia Highsmith, the accomplished practitioner of the psychological 'creepie'; and Christopher Lee, celebrated for his range of supernatural film roles, less well known as a scholar who was examined at Cambridge by M. R. James himself.

This entertaining but chilling anthology contains not only the winning entry – a hypnotic tale of a child's demon rituals with her dolls – but also the runner-up, two highly commended stories which were awarded special consolation prizes of £50 each, and a handful of the best from the several thousand sent in.

Apparitions, supernatural monsters and guilty projections from the subconscious abound in a prisoner-of-war camp, on a tropical island and in such frighteningly ordinary domestic settings that only the most brazenly insensitive will fail to find himself more than once glancing anxiously over his shoulder.

What the critics said (see over . . .)

'*The Doll Named Silvio* is a particularly gripping account of a young girl's unhealthy rituals with a large number of old dolls, which has all the qualities of a particularly disagreeable nightmare ... compulsive reading ... my favourite story was *The Harpsichord* ... told with insight and in a style that is quite charming. This is, indeed, a book that will give great pleasure and many of the stories will stand repeated reading.' Michael Wright, COUNTRY LIFE

'The standard is universally high and all the stories are readable.' – *Huddersfield Examiner*

'A must for all devotees of the genre ... most of them, though not necessarily the winning story about a strange girl and her crazy dolls, will scare the pants, or whatever, off.' WESTERN MAIL

'*The Doll Named Silvio* is certainly a real find – a hypnotic piece ... I very much admired Francis King's story, *A Scent of Mimosa*, quiet, elegiac, but subtle enough to freeze the most sophisticated blood.' – *Robert Nye, The Guardian*

'Nicely calculated to make any sensitive reader's flesh creep ... Out of an obvious embarrassment of riches the judges of the competition have picked some really first-rate tales of this particular genre.' CHURCH TIMES

The Times Anthology of Ghost Stories

CORGI BOOKS
A DIVISION OF TRANSWORLD PUBLISHERS LTD

THE TIMES ANTHOLOGY
OF GHOST STORIES

A CORGI BOOK 0 552 10474 4

Originally published in Great Britain by
Jonathan Cape Ltd

PRINTING HISTORY
Cape edition published 1975
Corgi edition published 1977

This book is set in Intertype Times

Corgi Books are published by
Transworld Publishers Ltd,
Century House, 61–63 Uxbridge Road,
Ealing, London W5 5SA

Made and printed in Great Britain by
Cox & Wyman Ltd, London, Reading and Fakenham

CONTENTS

PUBLISHER'S NOTE

The thirteen stories in this book were selected from several thousand entered in a ghost story competition organized in the spring of 1975 by Jonathan Cape in conjunction with *The Times* newspaper. The judges of the competition were the novelists Kingsley Amis and Patricia Highsmith and the actor Christopher Lee, together with John Higgins of *The Times* and Tom Maschler of Cape. The first prize went to Michael Kernan for his hypnotically terrifying *The Doll Named Silvio*, while the elegiac *A Scent of Mimosa* won second prize for Francis King; the highly commended stories of F. Terry Newman (*Marius*) and Sir Laurence Grafftey-Smith (*The Locket*) were awarded special consolation prizes.

MARIUS THE DOLL

by F. Terry Newman

'HELLO there, Pierre!'

The old Breton farmer paused under the laden apple-trees, and when he continued through the lush grass the swishing of his sandalled feet merged with the soft gurgling of the stream skirting the orchard.

Presently he stood over me, forefinger and thumb kneading his grizzled moustache, staring in abstracted wonderment at my canvas. He said, 'The painting, it goes well?'

Overhead the sky was cloudless, and already festoons of gnats shimmered and gyrated beneath the branches of the fruit-trees. When Marius appeared, moving silently among the limed, gnarled boles of the trees, we could see how he held the doll tightly in the crook of his arm. A shaft of sunlight, russet warm, slid over his wan face and he hesitated for a moment, watching us. Then the doll's legs dangled and jerked behind him as the boy's slight figure turned off towards the path leading back to the house. I laid my brush on the trellised table and leaned back in the canvas chair.

'Come on, Pierre. Tell me about him.'

'There is little to tell, Monsieur Peter, and all of it is sad.' His teak-calloused hands fluttered expressively. 'His parents were killed; his little sister, too, about two and a half years ago. But it was the war which killed them.'

'Two and a half years ago? The war's been over a long time now.'

Pierre Briand's shoulders lifted. 'For some, the war has never ended. They were in a motor launch, his mother and father, his sister Yvette, and Marius. Coming back from Granville, in Normandy. There was a mine drifting in the Rance estuary, near Dinard . . .'

'The Rance? Oh, yes! This stream flows . . .'

Pierre jerked a thumb. 'It is a tributary, a little one; about another eleven kilometres before it joins the river.' He shuffled round until he was facing me from the side of the easel. His grey eyes softened. 'The boy recovered quickly, the others were all killed. But the shock affected him, as you see. He is what you would call . . . strange. He was to be taken to a home for such unfortunates, at Brest; but Marie – my wife – she has a soft heart'.

'You adopted him?'

Pierre nodded. 'Marius Briand. He has our name.'

'Yet you said nothing about him when I wrote you from St. Helier.'

The Frenchman fumbled in the pocket of his baggy cardigan. 'But should I have done?' He made as if to offer the horn snuffbox, hesitated, took a generous pinch between thumb and forefinger and completed the ritual deftly and with satisfaction. 'You asked only if you could come and paint. You too have unhappy recollections of the war.' His eyes went to my extended leg and the stick lying on the grass. 'We have a sympathy for you.'

'I know you do, and I appreciate it. You've been very kind.'

Pierre shrugged. 'You know you are free to come and go when you wish.'

'But the doll he carries about, everywhere. That's strange . . . for a boy.'

'It belonged to Yvette, his little sister. But I do not know why he calls it Marius, his own name. Perhaps it was she who named it after her brother.' Pierre thrust his hands deep inside the pockets of his trousers and shrugged. 'I think, perhaps, it was at that time a very beautiful doll, made for Yvette by a craftsman at Limoges. It was said he moulded the face to resemble her mother but I think for the boy it typifies them both, for the face of the mother was also that of the daughter. His father, like you, was an artist.'

I smiled. Pierre was not usually so loquacious. 'Only a dilettante I regret, though now' – I reached down and tapped my game leg – 'I try to make up for time lost.'

'As you say – it is all so strange. But now' – he glanced upwards and turned towards the house – 'We wish to sell these apples, but not for cider, and they will soon be falling. I must get some baskets.' His quick grin revealed broken teeth the colour of old ivory. 'For you the painting – for me, the pulling.'

'Perhaps I can help a bit. Not a climbing man any more, but I'm not so decrepit I can't reach some of the branches.' But the old man was already off among the trees.

I picked up my brush and re-routed a spider which, with a leg it had trailed through the burnt umber, was tracing cabalistic patterns along the side of my palette. From my chair I was able to see across the stream the rich folds of countryside flanking the little village of Pleurtuit, and about a mile to the right of the river estuary, the walled town of St. Malo. Here at the edge of the orchard the branches hung low, framing the pattern of landscape I endeavoured to convey on to canvas.

Pierre returned with four wide-bottomed hazel-wood baskets, then disappeared again towards the house. Presently he returned with a ladder. I turned to watching him guiding its head dextrously upwards through the laden branches, stamping hard on the treads to secure a firm foothold.

Presently Marius appeared with another basket. He was wearing a pale blue-and-white-striped jersey with faded blue linen shorts, and his small puckered face was alight with anticipation. He hovered for a while near the baskets Pierre had piled on the grass, and when the old man went over to them I heard him remonstrating with the boy.

I returned again to my picture, but without enthusiasm. True, I had caught the rich colours, the luminous green of near hills, the blue of far ones, yet in this brilliant light it was something any colourist could have done. Years ago I had sold a few canvases of still life; it had led to adventures in the Impressionist school, whose various disciples had confused rather than given purpose to my vision. Then for a year I worked at portraiture, discovering Expressionism, most vital of all forms of aesthetic appreciation, where the painting can render visible the inwardness of personality. Now it was landscape. I had concluded that the surest way to discover one's real métier was to go through the whole gamut – a process of elimination.

Like the rebellious Franklin Watkins, one of the great portrait-painters of America who was also a painter of refreshing still-lifes, I too was consumed with an urge to seek new forms of expression outside the disciplined channels of convention. Like the Philadelphian rebel I too was a shirt-sleeved artist, assimilating the old wisdom, discovering paradoxically that there is nothing fresh to communicate unless it is already known. Of them all, I ruminated, portraiture had come closest to satisfying my flair for detail and characterization; for the Expressionist artist's task is not to render the already visible externals of life, but to make visible the inwardness both of his feelings and the things that excite him.

I leant back in my canvas chair, whilst hot rapiers of sunlight thrust through the branches, pricking my eyes with their intensity, and myriads of insects set the air throbbing with intense life. I complimented myself that here I had found one of those rare backwaters of peace which were becoming increasingly difficult to discover.

A startled cry and a sudden crash of branches broke my reverie, and swinging about I saw Marius suspended by one hand from a branch and the other clutching frenziedly at his doll. He was lunging, kicking out desperately with alternate feet in an attempt to secure a foothold, but his strength was unequal to the effort. I had almost reached him when he crashed through the branches to the ground. I could hear

Pierre shouting querulously and as the boy scrambled to his feet he came loping towards us. Marius pulled a grubby handkerchief from the pocket of his shorts and busied himself wiping the face and limbs of his doll. He seemed quite unhurt.

When Pierre reached us he protested volubly in his rich patois, his loquacity ineffectually concealing his fear for the boy's safety. Marius backed away, stumbling against his upturned basket and spilled fruit. Mutely he stared from me to his harassed foster-parent, automatically conveying the doll to his other hand and tucking its legs beneath the crook of his arm. Pierre shrugged and turned to me.

'Never for one moment,' he expostulated, 'will he put down that wretched *poupée*. That was why I cautioned him to pick only those apples he could reach, not to climb the trees. Marie would tear my entrails out if anything happened to the boy.' Again he shrugged, palms lifted entreatingly. 'What can I do? *C'est difficile* – I cannot be always at his side.'

The boy remained silent, shuffling uncomfortably at being the focus of attention. He moved into a patch of sunlight, the wide, dark eyes travelling from Pierre's face to my own, studying our expressions, then turned intently to the doll. Suddenly he uttered a low wail, a strange poignant cry which startled us both. It was like the cry of a trapped beast in the night. Marius was pointing to the doll's leg and then one of the arms, his finger trembling. When I moved closer I could see where some of the colour had been scraped from the wrist, and on the right leg there was an uneven scratch from knee to ankle. Marius kept a tight hold on the doll but it was my first opportunity of examining the strange figure upon which he lavished so much tenderness. I wondered if by some uniquely vicarious projection the doll which Yvette had named after him had become to Marius a personification of his lost sister.

I was more impressed by its meticulously lifelike features and craftsmanship of construction than its superfluous injuries, though to Marius it was obvious they appeared devastating. It was an excellent example of a French craftsman's work. Machine-made of Parian ceramic but hand finished with jointed limbs anatomically accurate and lifelike. It was dressed in a blue pinafore skirt and peach blouse, with a head of real auburn hair and unusual olive-grey eyes. The feet were encased in trim black leather shoes. When I examined the eyes closely I saw they were inset and of painted glass. The partially glazed cheeks held a realistic flush against a veiled pallor resembling incredibly the features of the boy himself.

'Why, Marius . . . that's a splendid doll!' I tried to make my voice soothing, casual. He gazed at me, a single tear welling from the corner of an eye. 'And those few scratches don't amount to anything. Won't you let me see to it for you? A touch of paint and it will be like new.'

The boy shook his head and moved away. His hands smoothed the creased garments. He fondled the pillowed head, picking a fallen leaf from the reddish-brown hair. I saw his teeth close abruptly over his lower lip and he winced when he wiped away the dirt from the stained limbs. I glanced at Pierre, who hunched his shoulders and lifted a hand, turning his wrist so that the palm was upturned. He shook his head uncomprehendingly. Very quietly Marius slipped away among the trees.

'You see how it is.' Pierre's grey eyes mirrored his frustration. 'We can't get near him . . . he lives in a world of his own. Only, sometimes, Marie is able to talk with him a little. Yet in his own way I suppose, he is a good boy.'

I helped to collect the apples which had spilled from Marius's basket, patently aware of the undercurrent of affection, even devotion Pierre felt for the strange child he had succoured.

The following morning I took with me into the orchard a copy of François Dumont's portrait of Mlle de Bethisy, a reproduction of the superb miniature from the Pierpoint Morgan collection in New York. It was my first attempt at serious copying and I found the punctiliously small scale of the work both challenging and fascinating. I was aware of Pierre diligently gathering fruit further down the bank of the stream and was too engrossed to spare him any attention; when I did lean back at last to assess my work in perspective I was almost complacently satisfied. True, it was but a copy of a copy on a six- by eight-inch board, yet I was conscious of an elation quite out of proportion to my achievement and singularly aware of a growing realization that at last I was discovering my true *forte*. Here surely was the true marriage of fine detail and realistic colouring – the miniature!

Marius's shadow falling across the edge of the picture disturbed my mood of self-congratulation. He must have been watching from close by, for when I turned he resumed his way with a barely perceptible limp towards the stream. I reached for my stick, welcoming the opportunity to stretch my limbs. 'Marius!' I called, hobbling after him through the rank grass.

Usually he would have melted elusively away but today he permitted me to approach without any outward sign of temerity, and almost at once I noted the inflamed weal on his wrist. On his right leg, too, faintly but easily discernible, was the scar of a partially healed wound. I was certain that the day previously he had borne no such injuries; yet, strangely, the long scratch on his leg was almost healed over.

I pointed to the leg, then to the overhanging branches. 'Been picking more forbidden fruit, Marius?' He took a pace backwards and remained shuffling nervously, eyes questioning; then his head inclined to one side, a spontaneous smile transforming his expression. He came forward almost eagerly, holding the doll out as though inviting my inspection. For a moment I stood puzzled and when I reached out for the doll he drew it back towards him; then, as though in some way my hesitancy had conveyed reassurance, extended it again balanced carefully upon both small hands.

'You see . . . Marius' – his quick glance darted up at me –

'but now she is good again.' He spoke in the slow, slurred patois of the region and it was the first time I had heard him speak. His expression of happiness was touching.

And now for the first time I was holding his precious doll in my hands, palpably aware of the boy's tenseness as he stood like a coiled spring waiting for my examination to end. I was impressed once more by the lifelike expression and realistic colouring. It was very much like holding a tiny sleeping child. Only then did I observe the reason for Marius's elation. The injuries of yesterday had disappeared. I peered closely at the wrist and leg. There was absolutely no mark on either limb.

'But how . . .?' I began lamely. Marius reached out without waiting for me to finish. Urgently, yet with consummate tenderness, he took the doll in his arms. I noticed his slight limp as he wound his way among the trees, the doll pinioned in the crook of his arm as one would hold a small dog. A sense of happiness seemed to radiate even through the back of his striped jersey.

Further down the bank of the stream I could hear Pierre setting his ladder against a tree, and I decided I would go along presently and tax him with the mystery. Why was Marius limping? How did he come to bear stigmata-like on his own limbs the scratches and abrasions of the doll? What caused the marks to disappear from the doll, as though they had healed . . . from within?

I am familiar with only one satisfactory therapy for problems which set the brain swimming in abortive circles. I went back to my canvas chair. And soon I was engrossed. Yet frequently, despite my absorption, the face of Marius the doll, inanimate yet strangely alive, intruded; materializing for a few seconds, an amorphous mist between brush and the board on which I worked, then presently dissolving so that the face of Marius the boy, living yet passionless, as though the spirit was remote, withdrawn, would take its place.

It was as though there existed an indefinable rapport between them and my picture – the portrait of Mlle de Bethisy. The colouring, perhaps. Luminous, with highlights which softened and changed with every gradation of light, holding the illusion of depth, dimension. Beneath the cheekbones the soft concavities were so real it seemed a forefinger could trace the gentle undulations. The pigment was the hue of living flesh, warm-textured, and on the gently curving upper lip the subtlest intimation of soft down. I wondered whether it was due entirely to my own skill or whether some fortuitous combination of light and pigment had endowed it with a magic of their own. Though whether it was the face of Marius which it resembled or that of the doll I was unable to determine. Here, in Pierre Briand's orchard in tranquil Brittany, in this quiet backwater of the Rance, I was confronted with an enigma mysterious and baffling. I decided that at the first opportune moment I would try to win Marius's confidence. Perhaps I could draw him out, coax him to confide in me.

That night in my little room, between sheets that smelled faintly of sandalwood, gazing at the familiar prints, the fleur-de-lys patterned wallpaper and the painted plaster Madonna in its niche by the door, I elaborated the questions I would put to him on the morrow. In the adjoining room Marius slept peacefully.

The next day I made a discovery; ordinary enough in the general run of things, but significantly important to me. In one of Pierre's old books I found the faded colour print of a Greuze miniature. A picture of Jean Baptiste's daughter. I drew his attention to it. With wry humour he tore it from the book, grinned, shrugged and thrust it into my hand. I pinned it to my easel. Here was another challenge. To recreate on the same small scale the exquisite likeness with which Greuze had delineated Baptiste's own child. Chocolate-box school or not, it was an enviable composition. I quite forgot about Marius.

When the boy's sudden cry stabbed the quiet peacefulness of the morning I was vaguely conscious of irritability. It came again then, repeated faintly before breaking off abruptly and jerking me back to reality. It sounded like a cry for help and came from the far end of the orchard.

One side of the irregularly shaped holding sloped down to the water's edge. At the southern extremity an out-thrust of the bank, a small promontory, extended almost a third of the stream's width. As I drew near I could hear the threshing of water and loped along as fast as my game leg would allow, until at a bend in the stream I could distinguish Marius lying full length on the bank. His head was facing the stream and with both hands he was making frantic efforts to regain something floating just beyond his reach. At that moment, as though realizing the futility of his efforts, he sprang to his feet and took a few paces backward, and as I came up with him was about to leap into the stream. I grasped the back of his jersey and as he turned a startled, tear-stained face caught a glimpse of his doll. Half submerged, it spun and twisted in a miniature vortex in deep water in the lea of the projecting bank.

Marius nearly pulled me into the water as he lunged forward again. I tugged angrily at his jersey and grabbed one of his arms, forcing him to kneel at my side as I lay full length on the bank. Then I stretched the crooked handle of my stick out towards the doll. I got soaked to the shoulder in my efforts to reach out far enough to hook the bedraggled figure, and once, when I did get a slight purchase on it, Marius leapt at my arm with such vehemence that the doll freed itself and disappeared under the water.

It required most of my attention to restrain him from jumping into the stream, and only after repeated efforts when I managed to hook the doll beneath an arm did he quieten, trembling and biting his lip as I drew it carefully towards the bank. Marius clutched at it, hugging the drenched figure to his body as he sprang to his feet, and then with a quick glance of gratitude raced off towards the house.

I peeled off my jacket, wrung out the soaked sleeve and laid it in a patch of sunshine to dry. Then I returned to my painting. The sultry dark eyes of Jean Baptiste's daughter seemed to stare back at me with the same apprehensive gratitude as those of Marius. Or was it the doll?

I saw no more of the boy for the rest of the morning and imagined him tending his beloved, bedraggled doll. I presumed it best to say nothing to Pierre unless he referred to the incident. Marius was able to create enough troubles for himself without any assistance from me, and in any case they would see the sodden puppet. But when after tea that afternoon there was still no sign of him I taxed Marie about his absence.

'But he is in bed, Monsieur. He is sick, very sick.' Marie's rheumy blue eyes were haunted with fear. 'The doctor is coming up from Pleurtuit. His temperature, it still rises. *Alors!*' Her hands fluttered like the wings of a bird. 'We are *désolé*!'

I told her of the doll incident.

'I have been helping him to dry it, but she is much damaged by the water. We are very grateful to you.'

'He told you about it?'

She nodded. 'But yes.'

'But why, Marie? Why should Marius be . . . why should he be taken sick? He didn't go and fall in himself, afterwards?'

'*Mais non, Monsieur!* Only one of his sleeves was wet. Until the doctor comes we are no wiser than yourself.'

M. de Warren was one of the old school of family doctors. Physician, friend, and sometimes priest; as much a part of the surrounding countryside as the old elms crowding the banks of the Rance down to Pleurtuit. His leathery features were lined and drawn, his goatee, pewter-grey and square-clipped, invested his frail figure with an air of old world distinction. His diagnosis was summary and precise. Marius was suffering from a severe chill, and there were symptoms of nervous shock. The boy must be kept in bed with plenty of hot-water bottles. There were tablets to be administered every four hours until he called again the following morning.

But at the next visit the doctor spent a long time in the

boy's bedroom. I had finished my breakfast when he came out. His expression was grave. The resultant conversation with Pierre and Marie was conducted in undertones and lasted a long time. When he had gone they came back into the room. Their faces appeared drained of expression.

Pierre answered my unspoken entreaty. 'Pneumonia. The doctor says the boy must have fallen into the stream.'

'But he didn't,' I protested. 'His clothes were dry enough when Marie put him to bed – except for a sleeve.'

'That we cannot understand.' Pierre's voice was resigned; he shook his head. One gnarled hand went out and rested very lightly on Marie's shoulder. 'It is strange that he should have pneumonia.'

That afternoon Marius's condition remained unchanged, but towards evening he lapsed into a light coma. Looking into Marie's pain-saddened eyes as she informed Pierre of her intention to spend the night by the boy's bedside I felt humiliated by my own physical inadequacy; the realization that any urgent call for medical help must devolve upon the efforts of a care-worn man double my age.

Pierre spent some time working on his bicycle, then he charged the acetylene lamp with crystals of carbide and wheeled it down the garden path, leaving it by the gate ready for immediate use. An atmosphere of constraint seemed to settle over the old cottage, as though the years of summer sunshine stored in the mellowed red brick and uneven lichened tiles were being dissipated by sadness and melancholy.

I watched the old man pottering around the stove, and when he had heated some milk and taken a glass up to Marie I went over and stood for a while in the doorway. Night was already trailing an indigo backcloth over the distant fields of Britanny, and the walled town of St. Malo was silhouetted against the horizon like a steel-point engraving. The lights of Dinard flickered and scintillated, and at the mouth of the estuary pinpoints of light rode at the mastheads of the fishing boats.

Musing there, I recalled that occasion in the orchard when Marius had dropped his strange doll; how, at some mysterious and inexplicable psycho-physiological level its injuries had been transposed from the inanimate effigy to the boy who lavished upon it such an intensity of emotion. And I berated myself when the inspiration came for not thinking of it before. Quite suddenly it was obvious what I should do.

Pierre had returned from the bedroom and was sitting in his favourite chair by the window. I went over and placed a hand on his shoulder, and when he turned, looked up into my face questioningly, I pointed upstairs. He lifted his shoulders in assent.

Marie was seated on a low stool by the bed, her grey head nodding, when I tiptoed into the boy's bedroom. A single oil-lamp burned on the dresser, and in a tiny niche in the wall was a plaster-cast of the Virgin, a duplicate of the one in my own bedroom. I paused inside the doorway and when she made no move continued to the bedside.

The doll was lying on the coverlet with one of the boy's hands lying over it in an attitude of protection. Marius lay on his back, his breathing laboured and uneven. There were beads of perspiration on his forehead and his face was flushed with fever. He stirred, muttering unintelligibly, when I lifted his hand, but did not waken; and as quietly as I had entered I was able to steal out of the room without Marie being aware of my presence.

The doll was a woebegone caricature of the delicately beautiful figure I had known that sunny day in the orchard. The hair was a tangled mass, the clothes dishevelled and still damp. Most of the colouring had disappeared completely from the arms and legs, whilst one side of the tiny face was blotched and puce-coloured like the stained plaster of a dilapidated building. It was evident that the scheme I had evolved would be a great deal more difficult than anticipated, and had Marie queried my intentions at that moment I would have been at a loss to put them into words. I had expected the doll to have been damaged by the immersion, but not that the features would have been almost completely obliterated.

The little room Marie had designated for my own use contained the best illumination in the house. It was provided by a pressure-fed naphthalene lamp which gave a good even light, though for the task ahead of me it was woefully inadequate. Natural daylight would at least have given me an even chance. To make matters worse there was the innate conviction that I was working against time.

I primed the lamp first, then laid the doll on its side, bending it at the waist so that the lamp's heat would warm but not scorch the head and limbs. The selection and preparation of pigments took a long time and I mixed tempera with copal varnish to ensure a quick 'set' and promote colour fusion. And then, when the doll's limbs were thoroughly warm, I set to work.

It was an experience I shall long remember. The colours were absorbed as though a skin food was being applied to parched skin, and as I became engrossed a facility seemed to creep into my fingers such as I had never before enjoyed. There were moments when I had the peculiar feeling of being watched. Twice I was prompted with a strange and authoritative compulsion to select colours which, even as I mixed them, resolved into hues incredibly more appropriate than those I had been about to use. The flesh tones blended with almost eerie exactitude. As I handled the doll it was almost as though a sensation of life and vitality began to surge through the renovated limbs; as if at any moment the heat of the lamp might set a warm pulse beating.

The face was the supreme challenge, for I had less than half of the original from which to copy, and that stained and faded. Following as far as possible the exact positioning of the remaining features I outlined the brows and eye, applying middle tone over the whole area, painting in the iris while still wet and blending the edges with my finest sable; then the olive-grey pupil, and on completion a subdued highlight to the iris. The water-damaged eye I treated similarly with the pigments thinned.

The mouth was difficult. On such a small figure hard contouring would have given a 'painted on' appearance, but presently I was able to achieve a soft transition between the lips and surrounding flesh tones so that when completed it was extraordinarily natural. So remarkable that once again as I looked down on the doll it appeared to be imbued with life, the gently parted lips bearing the shadowy indentations of sentient flesh.

Perhaps it was the way I had been handling it, the heat of my hand: but the hair, tangled and unkempt when I had taken the doll from the boy's bed, was now smooth and shining as though recently brushed. I was surprised too that the diminutive skirt and blouse had not suffered from the immersion, being neither faded nor stained, whilst the black leather shoes were as neat as if they had been freshly polished. For some reason this untoward transformation made me feel a little uneasy; especially so, for at this moment my feelings were crystallized by a sound oddly resembling a sudden intake of breath seeming to come from behind my shoulder.

I waited an hour, and then with an impatience grown so intolerable I found myself trembling, another hour. It was enough, I decided. Though an appreciable time would have to elapse before the pigment hardened the surface appeared quite dry. I felt very proud.

Carefully I carried the doll back to Marius's room and laid it on the bed close to his side. Marie, wakened from her doze and still rubbing her eyes, was moving her stool to a position nearer the head of the bed. She stared at the transformed doll and her mouth opened. She pressed two fingers over her lips. And gazing down at the doll by the sleeping boy's side I realized that at last my métier was resolved – that I should paint miniatures.

And then, as if to resolve any doubts I may have had on this score, I saw the tear. A shining, pendulous globule, suspended from a corner of one of the freshly painted eyes, reminding me of a similar tear I had once seen brimming from Marius's eye. Instinctively, though logic affirmed it could be merely moisture drying out, I felt it was a tear of gratitude, not sorrow; and I was a little afraid. I stared into Marie's bewildered face, gave her a quick smile and went back to my room. Then I climbed into bed.

I dreamed that I was watching an artist at work, looking over his shoulder. When aware of my presence he turned to acknowledge me; I saw that his face bore a striking resemblance to that of Marius. When I heard the hammering on the door I opened one eye and saw that the spidery hands of the clock pointed to ten past eight. Moments later, when Pierre came bursting into the room, I knew what he was going to say without turning my eyes in his direction.

'The doctor,' he exclaimed excitedly. 'He has just been . . . the fever has gone. Marius is going to be well. And he is so different . . . you must see, come!' His face was radiant.

THE AXE

by Penelope Fitzgerald

... You will recall that when the planned redundancies became necessary as the result of the discouraging trading figures shown by this small firm – in contrast, so I gather from the Company reports, with several of your other enterprises – you personally deputed to me the task of 'speaking' to those who were to be asked to leave. It was suggested to me that if they were asked to resign in order to avoid the unpleasantness of being given their cards, it might be unnecessary for the firm to offer any compensation. Having glanced personally through my staff sheets, you underlined the names of four people, the first being that of my clerical assistant, W. S. Singlebury. Your actual words to me were that he seemed fairly old and could probably be frightened into taking a powder. You were speaking to me in your 'democratic' style.

From this point on I feel able to write more freely, it being well understood, at office-managerial level, that you do not read more than the first two sentences of any given report. You believe that anything which cannot be put into two sentences is not worth attending to, a piece of wisdom which you usually attribute to the late Lord Beaverbrook.

As I question whether you have ever seen Singlebury, with whom this report is mainly concerned, it may be helpful to describe him. He worked for the Company for many more years than myself, and his attendance record was excellent. On Mondays, Wednesdays and Fridays, he wore a blue suit and a green knitted garment with a front zip. On

Tuesdays and Thursdays he wore a pair of grey trousers of man-made material which he called 'my flannels', and a fawn cardigan. The cardigan was omitted in summer. He had, however, one distinguishing feature, very light blue eyes, with a defensive expression, as though apologizing for something which he felt guilty about, but could not put right. The fact is that he was getting old. Getting old is, of course, a crime of which we grow more guilty every day.

Singlebury had no wife or dependants, and was by no means a communicative man. His room is, or was, a kind of cubby-hole adjoining mine – you have to go through it to get into my room – and it was always kept very neat. About his 'things' he did show some mild emotion. They had to be ranged in a certain pattern in respect to his in and out trays, and Singlebury stayed behind for two or three minutes every evening to do this. He also managed to retain every year the complimentary desk calendar sent to us by Dino's, the Italian café on the corner. Singlebury was in fact the only one of my personnel who was always quite certain of the date. To this too his attitude was apologetic. His phrase was, 'I'm afraid it's Tuesday'.

His work, as was freely admitted, was his life, but the nature of his duties – though they included the post-book and the addressograph – were rather hard to define, having grown round him with the years. I can only say that after he left, I was surprised myself to discover how much he had had to do.

Oddly connected in my mind with the matter of the redundancies is the irritation of the damp in the office this summer and the peculiar smell (not the ordinary smell of damp), emphasized by the sudden appearance of representatives of a firm of damp eliminators who had not been sent for by me, nor is there any record of my having done so. These people simply vanished at the end of the day and have not returned. Another firm, to whom I applied as a result of frequent complaints by the female staff, have answered my letters but have so far failed to call.

Singlebury remained unaffected by the smell. Joining, very much against his usual habit, in one of the too frequent discussions of the subject, he said that he knew what it was; it was the smell of disappointment. For an awkward moment I thought he must have found out by some means that he was going to be asked to go, but he went on to explain that in 1942 the whole building had been requisitioned by the Admiralty and that relatives had been allowed to wait or queue there in the hope of getting news of those missing at sea. The repeated disappointment of these women, Singlebury said, must have permeated the building like a corrosive gas. All this was very unlike him. I make it a point not to encourage anything morbid. Singlebury was quite insistent, and added, as though by way of proof, that the lino in the corridors was Admiralty issue and had not been renewed since 1942 either. I was astonished to realize that he had been working in the building for so many years before the present tenancy. I realized that he must be considerably older than he had given us to understand. This, of course, will mean that there are wrong entries on his cards.

The actual notification to the redundant staff passed off rather better, in a way, than I had anticipated. By that time everyone in the office seemed inexplicably conversant with the details, and several of them in fact had gone far beyond their terms of reference, young Patel, for instance, who openly admits that he will be leaving us as soon as he can get a better job, taking me aside and telling me that to such a man as Singlebury dismissal would be like death. Dismissal is not the right word, I said. But death is, Patel replied. Singlebury himself, however, took it very quietly. Even when I raised the question of the Company's Early Retirement pension scheme, which I could not pretend was over-generous, he said very little. He was generally felt to be in a state of shock. The two girls whom you asked me to speak to were quite unaffected, having already found themselves employment as hostesses at the Dolphinarium near here. Mrs. Horrocks, of Filing, on the other hand, *did* protest, and was so offensive on the question of severance pay that I was obliged to agree to refer it to a higher level. I consider this as one of the hardest day's work that I have ever done for the Company.

Just before his month's notice (if we are to call it that) was up, Singlebury, to my great surprise, asked me to come home with him one evening for a meal. In all the past years the idea of his having a home, still less asking anyone back to it, had never arisen, and I did not at all want to go there now. I felt sure, too, that he would want to reopen the matter of compensation, and only a quite unjustified feeling of guilt made me accept. We took an Underground together after work, travelling in the late rush-hour to Clapham North, and walked some distance in the rain. His place, when we eventually got to it, seemed particularly inconvenient, the entrance being through a small cleaner's shop. It consisted of one room and a shared toilet on the half-landing. The room itself was tidy, arranged, so it struck me, much on the lines of his cubby-hole, but the window was shut and it was oppressively stuffy. This is where I bury myself, said Singlebury.

There were no cooking arrangements and he left me there while he went down to fetch us something ready to eat from the Steakorama next to the cleaners. In his absence I took the opportunity to examine his room, though of course not in an inquisitive or prying manner. I was struck by the fact that none of his small store of stationery had been brought home from the office. He returned with two steaks wrapped in aluminium foil, evidently a special treat in my honour, and afterwards he went out on to the landing and made cocoa, a drink which I had not tasted for more than thirty years. The evening dragged rather. In the course of conversation it turned out that Singlebury was fond of reading. There were in fact several issues of a colour-printed encyclopaedia which he had been collecting as it came out, but unfortunately it had ceased publication after the seventh part. Reading is my hobby, he said. I pointed out that a hobby was rather something that one did with one's hands or in the open air – a relief from the work of the brain. Oh, I don't accept that distinction, Singlebury said. The mind and the body are the same. Well, one cannot deny the connection, I replied. Fear, for example, releases adrenalin, which directly affects the nerves. I don't mean connection, I mean identity, Singlebury said, the mind is the blood. Nonsense, I said, you might just as well tell me that the blood is the mind. It stands to reason that the blood can't think.

I was right, after all, in thinking that he would refer to the matter of the redundancy. This was not till he was seeing me off at the bus-stop, when for a moment he turned his grey, exposed-looking face away from me and said that he did not see how he could manage if he really had to go. He stood there like someone who has 'tried to give satisfaction' – he even used this phrase, saying that if the expression were not redolent of a bygone age, he would like to feel he had given satisfaction. Fortunately we had not long to wait for the 45 bus.

At the expiry of the month the staff gave a small tea-party for those who were leaving. I cannot describe this occasion as a success.

The following Monday I missed Singlebury as a familiar presence and also, as mentioned above, because I had never quite realized how much work he had been taking upon himself. As a direct consequence of losing him I found myself having to stay late – not altogether unwillingly, since although following general instructions I have discouraged overtime, the extra pay in my own case would be instrumental in making ends meet. Meanwhile Singlebury's desk had not been cleared – that is, of the trays, pencil-sharpener and complimentary calendar which were, of course, office property. The feeling that he would come back – not like Mrs. Horrocks, who has rung up and called round incessantly – but simply come back to work out of habit and through not knowing what else to do, was very strong, without being openly mentioned. I myself half expected and dreaded it, and I had mentally prepared two or three lines of argument in order to persuade him, if he *did* come, not to try it again. Nothing happened, however, and on the Thursday I personally removed the 'things' from the cubby-hole into my own room.

Meanwhile in order to dispel certain quite unfounded rumours I thought it best to issue a notice for general circulation, pointing out that if Mr. Singlebury should turn out to have taken any unwise step, and if in consequence any inquiry should be necessary, we should be the first to hear about it from the police. I dictated this to our only permanent typist, who immediately said, oh, he would never do that. He would never cause any unpleasantness like bringing police into the place, he'd do all he could to avoid that. I did not encourage any further discussion, but I asked my wife, who is very used to social work, to call round at Singlebury's place in Clapham North and find out how he was. She did not have very much luck. The people in the cleaner's shop knew, or thought they knew, that he was away, but they had not been sufficiently interested to ask where he was going.

On Friday young Patel said he would be leaving, as the damp and the smell were affecting his health. The damp is certainly not drying out in this seasonably warm weather.

I also, as you know, received another invitation on the Friday, at very short notice, in fact no notice at all; I was told to come to your house in Suffolk Park Gardens that evening for drinks. I was not unduly elated, having been asked once before after I had done rather an awkward small job for you. In our Company, justice has not only have not to be done, but it must be seen not to be done. The food was quite nice; it came from your Caterers Grade 3. I spent most of the evening talking to Ted Hollow, one of the area sales-managers. I did not expect to be introduced to your wife, nor was I. Towards the end of the evening you spoke to me for three minutes in the small room with a green marble floor and matching wallpaper leading to the ground-floor toilets. You asked me if everything was all right, to which I replied, all right for whom? You said that nobody's fault was nobody's funeral. I said that I had tried to give satisfaction. Passing on towards the washbasins, you told me with seeming cordiality to be careful and watch it when I had had mixed drinks.

I would describe my feeling at this point as resentment, and I cannot identify exactly the moment when it passed into unease. I do know that I was acutely uneasy as I crossed the hall and saw two of your domestic staff, a man and a woman, holding my coat, which I had left in the lobby, and apparently trying to brush it. Your domestic staff all appear to be of foreign extraction and I personally feel sorry for them and do not grudge them a smile at the oddly assorted guests. Then I saw they were not smiling at my coat but that they seemed to be examining their fingers and looking at me earnestly and silently, and the collar or shoulders of my coat was covered with blood. As I came up to them, although they were still both absolutely silent, the illusion or impression passed, and I put on my coat and left the house in what I hope was a normal manner.

I now come to the present time. The feeling of uneasiness which I have described as making itself felt in your house has not diminished during this past weekend, and partly to take my mind off it and partly for the reasons I have given, I decided to work overtime again tonight, Monday the 23rd. This was in spite of the fact that the damp smell had become almost a stench, as of something putrid, which must have affected my nerves to some extent, because when I went out to get something to eat at Dino's I left the lights on, both in my own office and in the entrance hall. I mean that for the first time since I began to work for the Company I left them on deliberately. As I walked to the corner I looked back and saw the two solitary lights looking somewhat forlorn in contrast to the glitter of the Arab-American Mutual Loan Corporation opposite. After my meal I felt absolutely reluctant to go back to the building, and wished then that I had not given way to the impulse to leave the lights on, but since I had done so and they must be turned off, I had no choice.

As I stood in the empty hallway I could hear the numerous creakings, settlings and faint tickings of an old building, possibly associated with the plumbing system. The lifts for reasons of economy do not operate after 6.30 p.m., so I began to walk up the stairs. After one flight I felt a strong creeping tension in the nerves of the back such as any of us feel when there is danger from behind; one might say that the body was thinking for itself on these occasions. I did not look round, but simply continued upwards as rapidly as I could. At the third floor I paused, and could hear footsteps coming patiently up behind me. This was not a surprise; I had been expecting them all evening.

Just at the door of my own office, or rather of the cubby-hole, for I have to pass through that, I turned, and saw at the end of the dim corridor what I had also expected, Singlebury, advancing towards me with his unmistakable shuffling step. My first reaction was a kind of bewilderment as to why he, who had been such an excellent timekeeper, so regular day by day, should become a creature of the night. He was wearing the blue suit. This I could make out by its familiar outline, but it was not till he came halfway down the corridor towards me, and reached the patch of light falling through the window from the street, that I saw that he was not himself – I mean that his head was nodding or rather swivelling irregularly from side to side. It crossed my mind that Singlebury was drunk. I had never known him drunk or indeed seen him take anything to drink, even at the office Christmas party, but one cannot estimate the effect that trouble will have upon a man. I began to think what steps I should take in this situation. I turned on the light in his cubby-hole as I went through and waited at the entrance of my own office. As he appeared in the outer doorway I saw that I had not been correct about the reason for the odd movement of the head. The throat was cut from ear to ear so that the head was nearly severed from the shoulders. It was this which had given the impression of nodding, or rather, lolling. As he walked into his cubby-hole Singlebury raised both hands and tried to steady the head as though conscious that something was wrong. The eyes were thickly filmed over, as one sees in the carcasses in a butcher's shop.

I shut and locked my door, and not wishing to give way to nausea, or to lose all control of myself, I sat down at my desk. My work was waiting for me as I had left it – it was the file on the matter of the damp elimination – and, there not being anything else to do, I tried to look through it. On the other side of the door I could hear Singlebury sit down also, and then try the drawers of the table, evidently looking for the 'things' without which he could not start work. After the drawers had been tried, one after another, several times, there was almost total silence.

The present position is that I am locked in my own office and would not, no matter what you offered me, indeed I could not, go out through the cubby-hole and pass what is sitting at the desk. The early cleaners will not be here for seven hours and forty-five minutes. I have passed the time so far as best I could in writing this report. One consideration strikes me. If what I have next door is a visitant which should not be walking but buried in the earth, then its wound cannot bleed, and there will be no stream of blood moving slowly under the whole width of the communicating door. However I am sitting at the moment with my back to the door, so that, without turning round, I have no means of telling whether it has done so or not.

THE RESIDENT

by John Stevens

EARLIER this year, the Society of Ghost Writers held its first annual conference at Ruymp's Hall in Norfolk. And it proved to be an inspired choice of venue. All thirty or so of the Society's members were able to be present and it was possible to accommodate them very comfortably in the extensive seventeenth-century wing of the Hall which has often been attributed – quite erroneously, I must insist – to Inigo Jones.

Most of the members arrived in plenty of time to hear their President's address which, if subsequent comments are to be taken at their face value, was long, pompous and repetitious. I can certainly vouch for the fact that it went on for over an hour and a half, and that it took the form of a plea for a sustained corporate effort to achieve parity of esteem with other professional bodies. There was mention of course, of inflationary spirals and vortices, of devastating, eroding economic crises, of soaring costs of living. I found it dull, disappointing stuff; and I think there were plentiful signs that the members shared my feeling. But dinner in the Orangery did a deal to revive flagging spirits and to loosen tongues. Excellent food and splendid wines were served by a friendly and competent staff in elegant and impressive surroundings. And added to all this was the undoubted pleasure of meeting so many distinguished colleagues for the first time, of comparing notes with them on a whole range of fascinating topics of much concern to all the Society's members – scales of fees, the assessment of expenses, special charges for assignments of an unusual nature, retainers and refreshers.

The names on the members' lapel-badges were pseudonyms of course. How could it have been otherwise? The Society's very strict code of conduct demanded it. So too did the clients – many of them well-known public figures – on whom members depended for their livelihoods. There was Meredith Eliot, for example, who had just completed memoirs, running to four substantial volumes, for an eminent European statesman. Scott Austen, the Society's newly-elected Honorary Secretary, was responsible for the extensive literary output of an international pop-singer who had achieved stardom on the strength of electronically amplified monosyllables. Wodehouse Carroll, the Society's Honorary Treasurer, specialized in polishing the otherwise unreadable monographs of a famous art-historian to suit the coffee-tables of the well-to-do. His masterpiece was his transformation of the original *Medieval Masons' Marks* into *Erotic Graffiti of the Dark Ages*. In the latter version, lavishly illustrated, it achieved best-seller status in America.

The conversation of these three gentlemen – Eliot, Austen and Carroll – promised me both profit and pleasure. So I accompanied them from the dining-table to the library where they were delighted to discover a real fire, of genuine logs, burning on an undeniably authentic hearth. We occupied a semi-circle of splendid library chairs which stood there, ready to receive us.

Austen still had misgivings about the title chosen for the Society and feared that it might evoke a misleading image in the public's mind.

'After all,' he urged, 'it would do us no good at all to be confused with the hairy-hand brigade, with the scribblers of ghost stories.'

Carroll obviously shared his fears.

'I entirely agree,' he said. 'Personally, I should hate to be associated with insane laughter in the cellarage.'

'Or padlocks mysteriously removing themselves from coffin lids,' Austen added.

Eliot lay back in his chair so that the firelight produced a somewhat sinister glint in his eyes as he put a question to his colleagues.

'Assuming that the possibility of confusion exists ... and I gravely doubt whether it *does* ... what steps do you suggest that we take to avoid it?'

Austen concentrated on filling his pipe.

'What do you say to hyphenation?' asked Carroll.

'You mean Ghost ... hyphen ... Writer?' Austen inquired.

Carroll nodded.

'Well,' Austen conceded doubtfully, 'it's worth considering I suppose. But wouldn't a single word, a fully united word like Ghostwriter be equally acceptable?'

Eliot rounded on him furiously.

'No ... it ... would ... *not*!' he protested. 'Certainly not while *I* have anything to do with the Society. I should prefer to risk a degree of ignorant confusion than support any monkeying with established usage. I am frankly amazed by your suggestion.'

Austen, who was attempting to light his pipe, glanced up at his colleague apprehensively. Carroll did his best to create a diversion by indulging in a sort of private meditation. 'Trade-mark ... Turkey-poult ... Actor-manager .. Will-o'-the-wisp ... Conversation-piece ...'

Eliot snorted and rose abruptly to his feet. 'I wonder if the library boasts a Fowler,' he said.

He left us in order to search the shelves. When he had reached the far side of the library, Austen leaned confidentially forward in his chair, speaking in a low voice.

'Do you know Eliot well?' he asked.

I shook my head.

'Never met him till today,' Carroll said. 'But I've known him by repute for several years. Memoirs mostly, I believe ... And he has some pretty impressive clients, I'm told. I believe they include ...'

Austen cut short his companion's indiscretion.

'I have heard the list,' he said. 'And I agree that it's formidable. But I was less concerned with Eliot's reputation than with his appearance. I don't believe I've ever seen anyone so disconcertingly ugly. Have you?'

Carroll twisted himself round in his chair so that he could observe Eliot ferreting among the books.

'I can't say I had taken much notice,' he said.

Then he leaned forward urgently.

'My God,' he said. 'You are absolutely right! From this distance, and in this light, he scarcely looks human.'

Austen appeared relieved.

'I'm glad you agree,' he said. 'I thought at first that my eyes must be letting me down.'

'No, no,' Caroll assured him. 'It would require a robust constitution to withstand the shock of meeting our friend on a dark night.'

'Sinister, would you say?'

Carroll refreshed his memory with another look.

'Too mild,' he said. 'Malevolent?'

'He reminds me very much of Count Magnus,' said Austen.

We found ourselves watching Eliot with heightened interest as he stretched up to take a volume from a shelf that was strictly beyond his reach. A thin, dark arm emerged from the sleeve of his jacket almost as far as the elbow. His fingers flickered at the spine of the book so that, when he eventually contrived to dislodge it, it fell into his hands. He rapidly found the page he wanted and bore down on us with clear intent.

'Listen to what Fowler has to say on the subject of hyphenation. "The hyphen is not an ornament; it should never be placed between two words that do not require uniting and can do their work equally well separate." '

'Splendid!' said Austen.

Eliot sat down next to him and looked at each of us in turn over his gold-rimmed spectacles. His thick lips distorted themselves into a wintery grin.

'I suggest that we agree to leave the Society's title exactly as it is,' he said.

I noticed that Austen surreptitiously inched his chair closer to the fire in order to place a little more distance between Eliot and himself. Eliot obviously had more to say. He tapped the book on his knee to emphasize his point.

'The decline of literary standards in this country could undoubtedly be traced by anyone who cared to study the steadily increasing use of the hyphen as a meaningless decoration. The abuse amounts almost to promiscuity.'

Carroll grinned. 'Splendid subject for a doctorate thesis,' he suggested.

Eliot turned to him with an expression of quite awe-inspiring hostility. 'Perhaps,' he snapped. 'But it would require a Dietrich or a Furstheimer to attempt it. The subject is beyond the scope of the unimaginative, niggling, small-minded kind of so-called scholarship we encourage nowadays.'

Carroll nodded. Watching his gesture at close range, I found it ambivalent. Did it signify agreement or surrender? I glanced at Austen, who was preoccupied with his pipe. It appeared to be giving him a good deal of trouble. He huffed and puffed his way through almost a minute of frustration before getting up to knock out the ashes in the hearth. He turned to face Eliot with a friendly smile.

'When you read us your paper tomorrow morning,' he said, 'you will find yourself addressing no fewer than thirty-three ghosts. Thirty-four if you include our President.'

Carroll found the idea amusing. Eliot evidently did not.

'Well,' said Austen apologetically. 'We *are* ghosts of a kind aren't we? At least in a manner of speaking . . .'

There followed an embarrassed silence. Carroll did his best to break it pleasantly. 'What is your paper to be about?' he asked. Eliot's face was that of a very angry man. 'You mean you haven't taken the trouble to read your programme?' he demanded.

'Well, yes . . .' said Carroll. 'But . . .'

'If you had done so,' Eliot interrupted, 'you would have found that it incorporated an excellent summary of my paper. Members were expected to read the summary before coming to the conference.'

'I'm sorry,' said Carroll limply.

'It would seem that we have wasted a good deal of the Society's money on printing,' Eliot snorted.

'May I return Fowler to the shelf?' asked Austen, getting up from his chair and holding out a hand.

Eliot rose too. 'Thank you,' he said. 'But I am perfectly capable of returning it myself. Then I shall go down to the bar before it closes. And after that, I shall go up to bed. There are still one or two notes I must add to my paper before I shall be able to get any sleep.'

He left us abruptly and our gloom was at once relieved.

Carroll took plenty of time before speaking, allowing Eliot to remove himself from earshot. 'That,' he said with complete sincerity, 'is, without question, the most repellant-looking creature I ever clapped eyes on – as well as by far the rudest and the most uncouth.'

'Puzzling too,' said Austen. 'Who the hell are Dietrich and Furstheimer?'

Carroll shrugged. Austen transferred his question to me. I shrugged too.

'Eliot probably invented them,' said Austen. 'They sound ghastly enough to be the creations of his own repulsive imagination.'

'Feel like a drink?' Carroll asked.

I shook my head. Austen was more expansive.

'I'd sooner die of thirst than appear in the same bar as that fellow,' he said. 'Nothing will drag me into the place as long as *he's* there. Frankly, he gives me the creeps.'

Carroll hesitated before speaking. 'It's not just Eliot,' he said. 'It's the whole bloody place. I felt something queer about it the moment I saw it from the drive ... A sort of malaise which I can't explain. To be perfectly plain with you, I was sorely tempted to turn back.'

'What dissuaded you?'

Carroll considered his question. 'Let's say professional curiosity,' he said. 'First, I badly wanted to see what my fellow ghost writers looked like en masse, as it were. Second, I understand that there are some unusually diverting masons' marks in the chapel.'

'The chapel?' asked Austen.

'Late fourteenth century,' Carroll explained. 'Much the oldest surviving structure on the site. I have often intended paying it a visit ... and this seemed a useful opportunity. You see,' he went on, 'there's quite a demand for a sequel to the *Erotic Graffiti*.'

Austen paused in the act of lighting another pipe.

'I can well imagine it,' he said admiringly. 'And, by the way, does this place have a ghost? A proper bona-fide ghost of its own?'

'Not so far as I know,' said Carroll. 'Unless our friend Eliot is even more unpleasant than he seems.'

'Quite impossible,' said Austen with absolute confidence. Carroll seemed to be searching his memory. 'You mentioned a Count Magnus,' he said.

Austen nodded. 'Yes, I said that he reminded me of Eliot. Or vice versa. Don't you know him?'

'Never had the pleasure,' said Carroll.

Austen laughed. 'Pleasure!' he exclaimed, his eyes rolling in mock horror.

'The *other* kind of ghost?' Carroll asked.

'Horrible little devil. Central character in one of M. R. James's least probable stories.'

'I've never read them,' said Carroll. 'Ghosts aren't much in my line, to be honest. You may put me down as a complete sceptic.'

Austen looked provoked. 'I'm sorry,' he said, 'but I thought you said earlier that you felt uneasy in this place ... That you hesitated about coming in.'

Carroll laughed delightedly. 'Oh, *that*! I'm sorry if I misled you. But my reluctance had nothing whatever to do with ghosts. It's simply that I loathe these get-togethers. I'm not at all sure that I shall stay.'

Austen raised an eyebrow. 'Not even for Eliot's paper?'

'*Especially* not for Eliot's paper,' said Carroll. 'I think I shall content myself with a quick look at the chapel after breakfast. Then I'll be getting back to London.'

'By car?'

Carroll nodded. Austen grinned. 'Any chance of a lift?' he asked.

'Of course,' said Carroll. 'I'd be glad to help you escape.'

Austen pushed his long legs out in front of him towards the fire.

'Care to change your mind about that drink?' asked Carroll.

Austen looked at his watch. 'What about Count Magnus?' he asked. 'I've no wish to bump into him again tonight.'

'Oh, he'll have gone by now, surely,' said Carroll. 'He'll have gone up to get on with his damned paper.'

Austen got up from his chair. 'Very well,' he agreed. 'We'll try our luck.'

I anticipated his turn towards me.

'Would you care to join . . .?' he began.

I went on with my impression of someone who has dropped off to sleep. Apparently it was convincing.

'Forty winks,' said Austen.

I heard them moving towards the door.

'Quiet sort of chap,' I heard Carroll say. 'Do you know his name?'

'Can't say I do,' Austen admitted. 'Was he wearing a member's badge?'

The door closed behind them.

I enjoyed the luxury of having the library to myself. I liked Carroll and Austen; but enough is enough – even of good company. And I'm certainly nothing of a drinker; not any more. In the huge empty room the hilarities of the bar reached me only as a subdued murmur. Eventually, when the last drinkers had gone off to their beds, even the murmur gave way to silence.

I went to a window and drew back the curtains. It was a clear, cold night without a suggestion of wind to disturb the trees. A white mist lay over the ground like a coverlet. I returned to my chair to enjoy the last moments of the fire.

At ten minutes to one by the library clock, I decided that it was time for me to move. I walked through the Long Gallery as far as the main staircase. I climbed to the next floor which, only recently, had been divided in the most barbarous way to form a prodigious range of uncivilized guestrooms and bathrooms. In my candid opinion the architect should have been led to the wall of the stable court and shot without further ado.

Austen's room and Carroll's room were in darkness as I passed and I saw no reason to disturb them. But, when I observed the light under Eliot's door, I couldn't resist easing my way in to see what he was up to. He looked up as I entered.

I entirely agree with Austen. This fellow would serve as an excellent model for a portrait of Count Magnus – if only a sufficiently intrepid painter could be found. I left him with a mixture of astonishment and indignation on his revolting features. There might have been a suggestion – perhaps even more than a suggestion – of fear. I most devoutly hope so.

I adhered to my customary route, down the servants' stair and out into the south end of the colonnade. I crossed the old moat this side of the bridge so that I could pay due homage to the time-worn heraldic beasts along its parapet. I skirted the massive buttresses of the porch and finally entered the chapel through the full, formidable thickness of its towering east wall.

On the other side, I found myself hoping that Carroll, too, would find the wall intriguing, that he would be diverted by the cryptic marks of its builder as well as by the later, more overt, additions to its surface. And I gladly record that he *was*.

A SCENT OF MIMOSA

by Francis King

It was long past midnight when the municipal Citroën dumped the four of them outside the Menton hotel. Tom, the youngest and most assertive of the Katherine Mansfield Prize judges, grabbed Lenore's arm and helped her up the steps. It was Lenore, thirtyish and thinnish, who had that year won the prize, given by the municipality. Though they had never met until the start of their journey out to the South of France together, he was always touching her, as though to communicate to her some assurance, at the nature of which she could still only guess. As they followed behind, Theo and Lucy, the other two judges, maintained a cautious distance from each other. There had been some acrimony, many years before, about an unsigned review in *The Times Literary Supplement*. Lenore could no longer even remember which of the two had written it and which had felt aggrieved.

In the hall they all stared at each other, like bewildered strangers wondering what they were doing in each other's company so late at night, in an unknown hotel, in a foreign town.

Tom broke the silence, swaying back and forth on his tiny feet: 'Well, what's the programme for tomorrow? Christ, I'm tired!'

Lucy hunted for one of three or four minuscule, lace-fringed handkerchiefs in the crocodile bag that dangled from her wrist. When travelling with her stockbroker husband, she was used to more luxurious hotels, more powerful cars and more amusing company. 'Apparently we're going to be taken up into the mountains for another banquet.' She held the handkerchief to the tip of her sharp nose and gave a little sniff.

Theo, who was almost as drunk as Tom, wailed, 'Oh, God! Altitude and hairpin bends always make me sick.'

'Well, there'll be plenty of both tomorrow,' Lucy replied, with some relish.

Lenore gazed down at the key that she was balancing on her palm. 'The Ambassador told me that he would be placing a wreath on some local war-memorial. Tomorrow's armistice-day, isn't it?'

Lucy, who had been affronted that the prizewinner and not she had been seated on the New Zealand Ambassador's right, exclaimed, 'What a dreadfully boring man! Nice, but oh so boring!'

'Oh, I thought him rather interesting.' Lenore was still secretly both frightened and envious of Lucy, who was older, much more successful and much richer than herself. 'Some young New Zealander's going to meet us up there, the Ambassador told me. In the village. He's coming specially for the Katherine Mansfield celebrations.'

'I suppose if your country's produced only one writer of any note, you're bound to make a fuss of her,' Tom commented.

'Well, we'd better get some sleep. If we can.' Lucy began to walk towards the lift. 'The beds here are horribly hard and lumpy.'

Tom again held Lenore by the arm, as he shepherded her towards the small, gilded cage. So close, she could smell the alcohol heavy on his breath.

Lucy got out first, since on their arrival together she had managed to secure for herself the only room on the first floor with a balcony over the bay. Bowing to Lenore, she sang out, 'Bonne nuit, Madame la Lauréate!'

Lenore gave a small, embarrassed laugh. 'Goodnight, Lucy!'

Theo got out at the next floor, tripping and all but falling flat, with only Tom's arm to save him. He began to waddle off down the corridor; then turned as the lift-gates were closing. 'Bonne nuit, Madame la Lauréate!'

Lenore and Tom walked down their corridor, his hand again at her elbow, as though once more to assure her and perhaps also himself of something that he could not or dared not put into words. They came to her door.

'Well . . .' He released her and clumsily she stopped and inserted the key. 'Tomorrow we'll drive up into the mountains and watch poor Theo being car-sick and meet the Ambassador's young New Zealander. And, of course, hear lots and lots of speeches.'

She opened the door; and at once, as though frightened that she would ask him in, he backed away.

'Well, bonne nuit, Madame la Lauréate!'

'Bonne nuit, Monsieur le Juge!'

She shut the door and leant against it, feeling the wood hard against her shoulder-blades. Her head was throbbing from too much food and drink, too much noise and too much French, and her mouth felt dry and sour. What would each of the others be doing now that they had separated? She began to speculate. Well, Lucy would no doubt be taking great care of each garment as she removed it; and then she would take equal care of her face, patting and smoothing, smoothing and patting. Theo, drunken and dishevelled, his tiny eyes bleary and his tie askew, would perch himself on a straight-backed chair – he always seemed masochistically determined to inflict the maximum of discomfort on himself – and would then start work on the pile of postcards that he had rushed out to buy as soon as they had been shown into their rooms. The postcards would, of course, arrive in England long after his return. Someone had told Lenore that he had a wife much older than himself and a horde of children and step-children – six? seven? eight? – to all of whom he was sentimentally devoted. And Tom? Tom, she decided after some deliberation, would walk along to his room, wait there for a few minutes and then take the lift downstairs again and go out into the night, wandering the autumnal streets in search of a – well, what? She did not know, not yet; any more than she knew the nature of the assurance that constant touching was designed to convey.

The bed was soft, not hard and lumpy at all as Lucy had complained, too soft, so that its swaying was almost nauseating. Perhaps poor Theo would be bed-sick and would have to take to the floor ... She shut her eyes and yawned and yawned again ... She was asleep.

When she awoke, it seemed as if many hours had passed, even though the dark of the room was still impenetrable. Her body was on fire, the sweat pouring off it, her head was throbbing and she had an excruciating pain, just under her right ribs, as though a knife had been inserted there and was now being twisted round and round. The central heating was always turned too high in these continental hotels; and after having eaten and drunk so much, she ought not to be surprised at an attack of acute indigestion. She threw back the sheet and duvet and then, after lying for a while uncovered with none of the expected coolness, she switched on the bedside lamp and dragged herself off the bed. For a long time she struggled with the regulator of the radiator that ran the whole length of the window; but the effort only made her sweat the more, it would not budge. She would have to open the window instead. Again she struggled; and at last the square of glass screeched along its groove and she felt the icy air enfolding her body.

From her suitcase she fetched a tube of Alka-Seltzer and padded into the bathroom. It was as she was dropping two of the tablets into a tumbler of water, the only light coming through the half-open door behind her, that suddenly she felt a strange tickling at the back of her throat, as though a feather had lodged there, coughed, coughed again, and then effortlessly began spitting, spitting, spitting.

Giddy and feeling sick, the sweat now chill on her forehead and bare arms, she stared down at the blood that had spattered the porcelain of the basin and was even dripping from one of the taps. She felt that she was about to faint and staggered back into the bedroom, to fall diagonally across the bed, her cheek pressed against the thrown-back duvet. Oh God, oh God . . . She must have had some kind of haemorrhage.

She lay there, shivering, for a while. She would have to see a doctor. But how could she call one at this hour? The best thing would be to go along to the room of one of the others. But she shrank from appealing to either Lucy or Tom. It would have to be Theo.

She got off the bed, still feeling giddy, sick and weak, and went back into the bathroom to wash away the blood. This time she turned on the light. The two tablets of Alka Seltzer were now dissolved; but, with an extraordinary hyperaesthesia, she could hear the water fizzing even when she was still far away from it. She approached the basin slowly, fearful of what she would find in it: the trails and spatters of blood on the glistening porcelain and over the tap. But when she was above the basin and forced her eyes down, there was, amazingly, nothing there, nothing there at all. Porcelain and tap were both as clean as she had left them after brushing her teeth.

It was cold and damp by the mountain war-memorial, a lichen-covered obelisk, one end sunk into the turf, with a stone shield attached, bearing names that for the most part were Italian, not French. The Mayor, cheeks scarlet from the many toasts at the banquet and medals dangling from his scuffed blue-serge suit, stood before it and bellowed out an oration to which Lenore did not listen, her gaze tracking back and forth among the faces, mostly middle-aged and brooding, of the handful of villagers huddled about her. Lucy had retreated into the back of the municipal Citroën, saying that she was certainly not going to risk a cold just before she and her husband were due to set off for the Caribbean on a holiday. Theo was holding a handkerchief to his chin, as though he had an attack of toothache, his tiny eyes rheumy and bloodshot. Tom, who had been chatting to their dapper young chauffeur in his excellent French, now stood beside the man, faintly smirking.

At last the oration ended and the Ambassador, grizzled, grey-faced and grave, walked forward with his wreath, stooped and placed it against the tilted obelisk. An improbable girl bugler, in white boots and a mini-skirt that revealed plump knees at the gap between them, stepped proudly forward and the valedictory notes volleyed back and forth among the mountains. Again Lenore felt that tickling at the back of the throat; but now it was tears. She always cried easily.

Suddenly she was aware of a smell, bitter and pungent, about her; and she wondered, in surprise, what could be its source. It was too late in the year for the smell to come from any flower at this altitude; and it seemed unlikely that any of the village women – with the possible exception of the girl bugler – would use a perfume so strange and strong. She peered around; and then, turning, saw the tall young man with the mousy, closecropped hair and the sunburned face, his cheekbones and his nose prominent, who was standing a little apart from the rest of the gathering. A khaki rucksack was propped against one leg. Their eyes met and he smiled and gave a little nod, as though they already knew each other.

The ceremony was over. In twos and threes the people began to drift away, for the most part silent, and silent not so much in grief as in the attempt to recapture its elusive memory. The young man, his rucksack now on his back, was beside her.

'Hello.' The voice was unmistakably antipodean.

'Hello.'

'You won the prize.' It was not a question.

'By some marvellous fluke. I've never had any luck in my life before. Everything I've achieved, I've had to struggle for.' She gave an involuntary shudder, feeling the cold and damp insinuate themselves through the thickness of her top-coat. 'You must be the New Zealander.'

'*The* New Zealander? Well, *a* New Zealander.'

'We heard that you were coming.'

'I always try to come.'

The Ambassador was approaching, still grey-faced and grave. 'Your New Zealander has arrived,' Lenore called out to him.

'*My* New Zealander?' He looked at the young man, who held out his hand. The Ambassador took it. 'So you're from back home?'

The young man nodded, at once friendly and remote. 'Wellington.'

'What brings you here?'

'I wanted to be present at the ceremonies. I was telling Miss Marlow, I always have been.'

'Then you're a fan of K.M.?'

'Oh, yes.'

Lenore was becoming increasingly bewildered. She turned to the Ambassador. 'But didn't you say . . .? Didn't you tell me last night – at the banquet – that you were expecting a New Zealander?'

'I?'

'Yes, surely . . .'

'But I'd no idea that this young man would turn up, none at all.'

'But I'm sure . . . Didn't you . . .?'

'We've never set eyes on each other. And we know nothing about each other. Do we?' He appealed to the other man.

'Nothing at all.'

'Anyway' – cold and tired, the Ambassador began to move away – 'it's been nice to meet you. What's your name?'

'Leslie.' It might have been either surname or Christian name.

'We'll be seeing you again?'

'Oh, yes. I'll be at the prizegiving ceremony tomorrow. As I said, I've been at every one.'

Lenore and the young man were now alone by the lop-sided war-memorial. Far down the road she could make out Theo, shapeless in his ancient overcoat, a cap pulled down over his bulging forehead, as he urinated against a tree that soared up into the gathering mist and darkness. Tom was climbing into the car beside Lucy; Lenore could hear his laugh, strangely loud.

'How are you going to get down to Menton? Would you like me to ask if we can give you a lift?'

'Oh, that's very kind of you. But I think I'd like to stay here a little longer.'

'Here?' She could not imagine why anyone should wish to stay on in this cramped, craggy village, with all the inhabitants drifting back into their homes and nothing to see in the coagulating mist and dark and nothing to do.

He nodded. 'She came up here. She was driven up here by Connie and Jennie.'

'Oh, yes, they were the ones who let her the Villa Isola Bella, weren't they? Connie was the aunt.'

'Well, cousin really.'

'I didn't know she'd ever been in this village. I know the journals and the letters pretty well but obviously not as well as you.' Suddenly she did not wish to let him go; this imminent parting from a total stranger had become like the resurgence of some deep-seated, long-forgotten sorrow.'Can't we really give you a lift? We can squeeze you into our car.'

He shook his head. 'I want to stay here a little. But I'll be down. We'll meet again?'

'Perhaps this evening you might join us for dinner? We have the evening free and we thought that we might all go to a fish-restaurant in Monte Carlo. Lucy – she's one of the judges – says that Somerset Maugham once took her there and it was absolutely fabulous.' 'Fabulous' was not Lenore's kind of word; it was Lucy's. 'Do try to join us.'

'Perhaps.'

'Please! We'll be leaving the hotel at about eight-thirty. So just come there before that. It's the Hôtel du Parc. Do you know where it is?'

He nodded.

'How will you get down to Menton? There can't be a bus now.'

'Oh, I'll manage.'

'Lenore! Time we started back!' It was Tom's peremptory voice.

'I must go. They're getting impatient. Please come this evening.'

He raised his hand as she hurried away from him, in what was half a wave and half a salute. Then he remained standing motionless beside the war-memorial.

Lucy said fretfully, 'We want to get down the mountain before this mist really thickens.'

'I'm sorry. But that was . . . He was from New Zealand.'

'Is that the one you told us about last night?' Theo asked, wiping with a soiled handkerchief at eyes still streaming from the cold

Lenore nodded. 'Yes, I did tell you about him, didn't I?' She all but added, 'But the funny thing is that the Ambassador pretended that he'd said nothing to me at all about his coming.' Then something made her check herself.

It was as though, walking over sunlit fields, she had all at once unexpectedly found ahead of her a dark and dense wood; had hesitated whether to enter it or not; and had then turned and in panic retraced her steps.

'Well, he's obviously not coming.' Lucy drew her chinchilla coat up over her shoulders and got to her feet. The two men also rose.

Lenore sighed. 'No, I suppose not.'

'He probably decided there were more amusing things for a young man to do on the Côte,' Theo said.

'I can think of less amusing things too,' Lucy retorted tartly.

'Perhaps he hadn't got the money for a slap-up meal.'

Of course, of course! Tom was right. Lenore saw it now. What she should have said was, 'You must be my guest, because I want to spend some of my prize-money in celebration,' or something of that kind. She had spoken of the 'fabulous' restaurant to which Lucy had been taken by Maugham – enough to put off anyone who was travelling on a slender budget. Of course!

Once again Tom tried to take her arm as they emerged into the soft November air; but this time she pulled free with a sharp, impatient jerk.

The next morning they were driven out to Isola Bella, the villa on the steep hill where Katherine Mansfield had lived for nine months in a fever of illness and activity. The villa itself was occupied; but the municipality had made over a room on the lowest of its three levels into a shrine. A bearded French critic, who was regarded as an authority on the English writer, explained to Lenore that an outhouse had been converted into a lavatory and shower, in the hope that some other English writer might soon be installed in what was, in effect, a tiny apartment.

'But Katherine Mansfield herself never lived here?'

He hesitated between truth and his loyalty to his hosts. Then: 'Well, no,' he agreed in his excellent English. 'Katherine lived above.' (He invariably referred to the writer merely by her Christian name.)

'And probably she never even came down here?'

Again he hesitated. 'Possibly not.'

Lenore wandered away from the rest of the party, up the hill to the rusty gates that led to the main part of the house. Ahead of her, as she peered through the curlicues of wrought iron, stretched the terrace on which the invalid would lie out for most of the day on a chaise-longue spread with a kaross made of flying-squirrel skins brought home from Africa by her father. Oh, and there were the mimosa trees, like elongated ferns – Katherine Mansfield had described how she would lie awake at break of day and watch the shafts of the rising sun shimmer through them. All at once, Lenore could smell the tiny yellow flowers still hanging from the fragile racemes. Though infinitely fainter, a mere ghost, it was none the less that same odour, pungent and bitter, that had enveloped her up in the mountains. But surely, so high up in the mountains, no mimosa could grow or, if it did, could come to bloom in November? As she breathed in the scent, deeper and deeper until her lungs began to ache with it as they had done that first night in the hotel, she thought once again of the New Zealander and wondered what had happened to him. She had hoped to see him in the town early that morning as she had wandered alone about it, pretending that she was in quest of presents but in reality in quest of him; but he had been nowhere. And now he had not turned up at the villa, as she had also hoped that he would do. Perhaps he had already moved on, with his exiguous rucksack, farther up the coast; perhaps she would never see him again.

Suddenly she wanted a spray of the mimosa. She rattled the gate and the rusty padlock swung from side to side, with a dry sound of scraping against the bars. The occupiers of the house must be away. But she tugged at the bell, hearing it tinkle from somewhere out of sight. No one came. She thought, If he were here, he could climb over for me. He'd find some way. She hoisted herself up with both hands, feeling the flaking metal graze a palm. But it was useless.

'Can I help madame?'

It was the French critic, stroking his beard with a narrow, nicotine-stained hand.

Lenore explained what she wanted; and then he too tugged at the bell-pull and even shouted out in French. No one came. Oddly, she could no longer smell that pungent, bitter odour, not since he had come.

He shrugged. 'I'm afraid that I am too old and too fat to climb over for you. Perhaps if you come tomorrow, the owners will be here.'

'We're leaving tomorrow morning.'

'Then . . .' Again he shrugged. When he had first seen her, he had thought her a dowdy, insignificant little woman, and had hardly bothered to speak to her. But now he experienced a sudden pull, as though a boat in which he had long been becalmed had all at once felt the tug and sweep of the tide. Now he too grabbed her arm just above the elbow, as Tom had kept on doing until that rebuff of the previous night. 'Let me assist you down the hill.' How thin the arm was, how pathetically thin and fragile – the arm of a child or invalid. He felt excited at the contact.

'I have given most of my life to Katherine,' he told her, as they began to descend. It was not strictly true, since he had given much of his life to other things: to the editing of a magazine, to the collection of Chinese works of art, to women, to eating and drinking. But at that moment, when his fingers felt the delicate bone inside its envelope of flesh, he not only wished that it had been so but believed that it had been so. 'In a strange way you remind me of her, you know.'

In the town hall the audience for the prize-giving ceremony was composed almost entirely of elderly men in dark suits and elderly women in hats. Lenore had been told that she would have to make a small speech of thanks in French after Lucy had spoken, also in French, on behalf of the judges. Lenore had never made a speech in her life, let alone a speech in French, and she dreaded the ordeal. The hall was stuffy, its radiators too hot to touch even on this autumn day. She felt headachy, sweaty and vaguely sick, as she listened, in a kind of trance, first to the orotund platitudes of the Mayor, then to the clipped phrases of the Ambassador and finally to Lucy's few witty, lucid comments. In rising panic she thought, If he were here, if only he were here! In one hand she was clutching the typescript, the French of which Lucy had corrected for her.

She heard her name and then one of the French officials was giving her a little push from behind, his hand to her shoulder. She rose and, as she did so, she felt the room revolve first gently and then faster and faster around her. She clutched the back of her chair, staring up at the face of the Mayor on the dais above her. All at once she could smell, far stronger than ever before, that pungent, bitter odour of mimosa. It was all around her, an enveloping cloud. She moved forward and then up the steps, the French critic putting out one of those long, narrow hands of his to help her.

She was handed an envelope, cold and dry on her hot and damp palm and then she was handed a red-leather box, open, with a bronze medallion embedded in it. Whose head was that? But of course – it was Katherine Mansfield's, jagged prongs of fringe across a wide forehead. She looked down and read: 'Menton c'est le Paradis d'une aube à l'autre.'

The Mayor was prompting her in a sibilant whisper, perhaps she would wish to say a few words?

She turned to face the audience; and it was then, as she moistened her lips with her tongue and raised the sheet of typescript, that all at once she saw him, standing by himself at the far end of the hall, one shoulder against the jamb of a closed door and his eyes fixed on her.

She began to read, at first all but inaudibly but then in a stronger and stronger voice. Her French was all but perfect; she felt wholly calm.

In the premature dusk, they talked outside the Town Hall, pacing the terrace among the stunted oleanders.

'You saved my life,' she said. She felt the euphoria that precedes a bout of fever. 'I can't explain it but I was, oh, petrified, I felt sure I could not say a word, and then suddenly I saw you and all at once . . .'

'I like that story of yours. Very much.'

'Oh, have you read it?' She was amazed. The story had appeared in a little magazine that, after three issues, had folded and vanished.

'Yes. It was – *right*. For her, I mean. It's the only story that she herself might have written, of all the ones that have ever won the prize.'

'That's a terrific compliment.'

'I mean it.'

'I'd hoped that perhaps you'd have joined us last night.'

'Well, I wanted to,' he said, with no further excuse.

'And then I thought that I might see you at the villa.'

'I've been there many times.'

'But not this time?'

He did not answer; and then she began to tell him about the mimosa on the terrace – how she remembered reading about it in the journals and the letters and how she had wanted a spray, just one spray, but there had been no one at the house and the gate was padlocked.'If you'd been there, perhaps you could have climbed over. But none of our party looked capable of doing so.'

'I'll get you a spray.'

'Will you? Can you?'

'Of course.' He smiled. His teeth were very white in the long, sunburned face.

'But we leave early tomorrow.'

'What time?'

'We must leave the hotel at ten for the airport.'

'Oh, that'll give me time. Don't worry.'

Boldly she said, 'Oh, I wish there were no banquet this evening! I wish we could just have dinner alone together.'

'There'll be other times,' he said quietly. 'Anyway, I won't forget the mimosa.'

'Promise?'

'Promise.'

After that Tom was again calling and the cars were starting up and people were shaking her hand and saying how glad they were for her and that soon she must come back to Menton again.

When she looked round for the New Zealander, she found that he had vanished.

*

Lenore was back in her dark, two-roomed Fulham flat. At the airport Lucy had been whisked off by her husband in a chauffeur-driven Daimler, barely bothering to say goodbye. Theo had explained that it would be impossible to fit any more passengers into his battered station-wagon, already packed with his wife, a number of children, a dog and a folding bicycle. Tom had said that it looked as if the friend who was supposed to meet him must have got held up and he'd wait around for a while. So Lenore had travelled alone on the bus. She had felt chilled and there was again the pain, dull now, under her right ribs.

She shivered as she stooped to light the gas. Then she remained kneeling before it, staring at the radiants as the blue light flickering up from them steadied to an orange glow. He had failed to keep his promise and she had no idea of where he might be or even of what he was called – other than that either his surname or his Christian name was Leslie. It was hopeless. She got up, with a small, dry cough, and went into the bedroom. There she hauled her suitcase up on to the bed and began to unpack it, hurriedly, throwing things into drawers or jerking them on to hangers, as though she did not have a whole empty evening ahead of her and a number of empty days after that. At the bottom of the suit-case she came on the typescript of her speech – she crumpled it into a ball and threw it into the waste-paper basket – and the red-leather box, containing her trophy. She pressed the stud of the lid and lifted it upwards with a thumb; and, as she did so, it was as if she were releasing from it the smell pungent and bitter, that soon was all around her. She gave a little gasp; the pain in her chest sharpened. Looking down, she saw the spray of mimosa that lay across the medallion.

She took the spray in her hand; but it was dry, dry and faded and old as though it had lain there not for a few hours but for many, many years. 'Leslie.' She said the name aloud to herself and then, with no shock and no alarm but with the relieved recognition of someone lost who all at once sights a familiar landmark, she remembered that yes, of course,

Leslie had been the name of the beloved brother killed in the war, whom Katherine Mansfield had always called 'Chummie'.

She touched the arid, dead raceme and some of the small, yellowish-grey blossoms, hard as berries, fell to the carpet at her feet. They might have been beads, scattering hither and thither. Three or four rolled back and forth in her palm. She felt a tickle at the back of her throat; it must be pollen, she decided wrongly.

Then suddenly the concluding lines of Kathleen Mansfield's sonnet on the death of her brother, read long ago and forgotten, forced themselves up within her, like the spurs of a plant, buried for years, all at once thrusting up into the light of day,

> By the remembered stream my brother stands
> Waiting for me with berries in his hands . . .
> 'These are my body. Sister, take and eat.'

She gave another little dry cough, and tasted something thick and salt on her tongue. The scent of mimosa was already fading as those blooms had long since faded. But she knew that it would come back and that he would come back with it.

THE HARPSICHORD

A GHOST STORY FOR CHILDREN

by Elizabeth LeFanu

IT was a shattering blow. These were to have been the best summer holidays they had ever had. Alicia had arrived yesterday after her first term away from home and Giles was due tomorrow. Now here was Mother with a troubled face and a telegram in her hand, to say that Giles had been in contact with scarlet fever. That meant he must stay on at school for ten long days, 'Or else,' began Mother, and stopped.

'Or else what?'

'I could fetch him home by car and keep him in quarantine here for ten days, but that would mean packing you off somewhere.'

'Oh, couldn't we be in different parts of the house, and shout through the doors, and keep ten yards apart in the garden – or five yards–'

But Mother shook her head. 'No, it would be impossible,' and as she clearly would not give way on this point Alicia did not waste time in argument.

'Of course Giles must come home,' she decided. 'Now, where shall I go?'

'I'm sure Cousin Bee would have you. She's kindness itself and always says she doesn't notice one more among so many.'

Alicia considered it for a moment.

'Too much like school,' she said, 'without a minute to yourself.' After another pause for reflection she asked, 'Would Aunt Sophie have me?'

Mother looked surprised. 'Wouldn't it be a little dull, darling? They are both rather old and fragile.'

Alicia said 'I know – but they are very nice and reasonable, and they have a heavenly piano. I haven't had a chance to enjoy myself in peace with a piano for three months and that's what I want to do.'

There had been an allotted half-hour's practice daily at school, but with 'The Merry Peasant' prattling in the imperfectly sound-proofed cell to the right, and 'The Death of Ase' dragging on painfully to the left, Alicia could only struggle with the notes and do her best to drown them.

Mother arranged it all on the telephone, and she and Alicia drove off through the warm, still afternoon. Aunt Sophie was waiting for them in the coolness of her dark panelled hall, and Uncle Frederic emerged from his own room and blinked at Alicia in a very friendly way. They had a lady-like tea under the trees, not like their picnics at home, and Alicia felt it was all rather like a dream. Then Mother drove away, as she was going straight on to collect Giles, saying, 'We shall be over to fetch you in ten days from now, and I'll ring up and we can talk sometimes.'

Aunt Sophie, wearing a large shady hat, took Alicia round the garden, and told her she could come and pick the peaches and plums whenever she wanted to, and then she showed her her room and said it was such a pleasure to them both to have her there, and they hoped she would not be too dull.

Alicia unpacked her suitcase and came downstairs with all the music she had brought with her. She met Uncle Frederic in the hall and said, 'May I please play the piano? I haven't been able to play properly – I mean to wander about on the piano like I do at home – for months and months. And yours is such a heavenly piano.'

Uncle Frederic said, 'Oh dear, dear! Tut-tut, my dear child, this is most unlucky – how very unfortunate – Sophie, this is indeed a calamity. Here is Alicia with her music wanting to play – and the piano, dear child, has been found to have moth in it and has had just at this moment of all others to go to Mr. Bagenal to have the felts renewed. A charming man and a most excellent craftsman and a thorough musician – we could not wish for a better man. But it is most unlucky happening just now.'

Here was another bolt from the blue – two in one day. Poor Alicia was stricken. When she saw Uncle Frederic's face, quite pink with distress, she managed to say, 'Never mind, Uncle Frederic, it can't be helped.' But she felt the acutest disappointment and a sense of emptiness and frustration she could hardly bear. She escaped upstairs again, wondering how she was going to get through the next ten days, and almost regretted Cousin Bee's noisy party.

Without any particular motive she wandered up to the top of the house and looked into several unfamiliar rooms: they had a severe and withdrawn appearance and she felt rather shy of entering. A boxroom, with some old-fashioned pieces of furniture shrouded in dust-sheets, two cane trunks and a doll's house, was more inviting. Alicia thought this would be worth exploring later on – she did not feel the heart for it now, and in the hope of finding some books she went on down a short passage and a half-staircase and opened the door of a small white-panelled room.

The other rooms had seemed to repel her, but this room invited her in. There was a low window seat with bookshelves on either side, and she sat down and looked into the garden, with straight box-bordered paths and ripe peaches and plums on the walls. Beyond that were rolling fields and far away the faint contour of Salisbury Plain against the evening sky.

Alicia looked out of the window for a long time, then she began to look at the books in the shelves. There were some illustrated natural-history books that she liked very much, written in a polite and stilted manner but with beautiful, accurate pictures of flowers and birds. She pored over them until the fading light made it hard to see the small print – then she sat up and looked all round the little room. It was faded but very pretty, and Alicia felt at home there. She sat in the chairs in turn, looked in the mirror and then crossed the room to examine – what was it? It was made of light polished wood, inlaid with patterns of flowers, and it looked almost like – but it couldn't be – a piano?

Alicia tremblingly raised a polished lid – and saw two keyboards, one slightly above the other, with faded yellowish ivory keys, and one or two stops, like an organ, at the side. She struck a few notes and they sounded quite different from the notes of a piano – they had a bright glittering sound that was most exciting.

What can it be? thought Alicia. It's the most thrilling thing – you can play it like a piano, but it's quite different – more exciting – and lovely, too, though it's horribly out of tune. But why two keyboards and what on earth are these stops for? And the pedal – not like a piano pedal.

She pulled up a chair and tried playing bits of everything she could think of. Some went better than others. A Haydn minuet sounded more alive and sparkling than it ever had before— 'It might have been written for the thing, whatever it is,' cried Alicia: but when she tried 'The Death of Ase' on it, it made her burst out laughing. She was puzzled to notice a great black scar running across the polished wood, and the intricate inlay had been damaged, too – how and when she could not guess.

At last she heard sounds from the garden – she looked out of the window and in the dim light she could see Aunt Sophie and Uncle Frederic moving about the garden and calling her. 'Gracious, I've been here for ages! They must think I'm lost – perhaps they think I've run away.' Alicia felt her way up the little staircase and along the passages and raced downstairs, forgetting that she had felt very like running away when she climbed up them an hour or two ago.

'Aunt Sophie, Uncle Frederic, here I am! I've found the most extraordinary thing upstairs, in a dear little white room over the garden – I saw you out of the window – I'm sorry I've been so long, but I've been staying up there with my discovery. What is it? Like a piano – but not – with a lovely sound like gold wires.'

They looked relieved and bewildered; and now Uncle Frederic's face cleared and he said, 'My dear child, it's your great-great-grandmother's harpsichord. She played it very beautifully, I believe. It has always been kept in her own room, where she used to play it, and where you found it. Mr. Bagenal did it up for us many years ago and he comes sometimes to look after it. But a harpsichord goes out of tune very quickly and I fear it must be sadly out of tune now?'

'Yes it is,' agreed Alicia, 'but may I play it while I'm here, all the same? Oh, please say yes!'

'Yes, indeed you may. How glad I am you discovered it. But we will go tomorrow into Salisbury and try to persuade Mr. Bagenal to come back with us and put it into order, and he will I am sure tell you something about the instrument and how it should be played.'

After supper Uncle Frederic pointed to a picture on the drawing-room wall and said, 'This is your great-great-grandmother – she was Alicia, too, you know, and you were named after her.'

Alicia looked with interest and gave a cry of delight – 'Why she is playing the harpsichord – my harpsichord – in that very room.'

Aunt Sophie was looking from Alicia to the girl in the picture. 'My dear, you are very like her – look, Frederic, it's most curious. It has never struck me before – she is paler than you, of course, but the line of the forehead and cheek – and her hair – it's most striking.'

Uncle Frederic was looking too and nodding his head. 'And you are both musicians,' he said. 'I want to hear you play the harpsichord, Alicia, and bring it to life again.'

Alicia was intent on the picture. 'Who is this?' she asked, 'this man in black, with white hair, with his hand over his eyes, listening to the music?'

'We don't know his name,' replied Uncle Frederic, 'nothing seems to be known of him. He may have been her music-master. Rather a severe one, I should suppose. He looks a crotchety old gentleman, don't you think?'

Alicia looked closely at him. 'No, I don't think so, but he has a very sad face, and there's something about him I can't quite understand. I should like to find out.'

The next morning they set out to visit Mr. Bagenal, as Uncle Frederic had promised. He had not driven to Salisbury for some time and Aunt Sophie was plainly nervous of his doing so. She sat beside him, stiff and upright in her seat, and said, 'Slowly here, dear,' or 'Carefully please, Frederic,' at road-junctions and blind corners – although he was in fact driving both slowly and carefully, Alicia thought.

In the main street Aunt Sophie shut her eyes convulsively and opened them only when they reached Mr. Bagenal's shop. He proved to be as charming as Uncle Frederic had reported, and he showed Alicia a little clavichord, a virginals, which was like an oblong painted box placed on a table, and a fine harpsichord which he was doing up, and explained something of the differences between them. He allowed her to play on them and to compare the gentle tender tone of the clavichord and the pretty tinkling virginals (this might, he said, have been Queen Elizabeth's own instrument) with the more brilliant harpsichord. She was enthralled, and blushed with pleasure when she heard Mr. Bagenal tell Uncle Frederic that she played with real intelligence and musical feeling.

Mr. Bagenal shook his head when Aunt Sophie said she hoped they might have the Blüthner piano back in a few days for Alicia to play, and said it would be a matter of weeks, but he consented to come there and then to attend to the harpsichord.

So he drove back to lunch with them and answered Alicia's many questions with interest and good humour. Then she took him to the little white-panelled room, and while she watched him open up the harpsichord and adjust the jacks he told her a great deal about it, and spoke lovingly of the instrument for which Bach and Scarlatti and Couperin and Haydn wrote— 'Then Haydn *did* mean that minuet to be played on a harpsichord!' cried Alicia. He gave her a lesson in the use of the stops and the double keyboard and much else. He was as puzzled as she was by the great black scar across the instrument.

'It was the first thing I noticed when your uncle asked me to restore it, years ago now, and I've never been able to account for it,' he said. 'It looks almost as if the wood had been burnt – something has seared right into it, one can't imagine how. And look here – the ivory must have been broken off·two of the keys at the same time. You can see that it has been replaced – oh! probably as much as a hundred years ago – look, the ivory on these A and B keys is not quite so old and yellow.'

When Mr. Bagenal had gone (in a taxi – Aunt Sophie would not hear of Uncle Frederic driving into Salisbury again) Alicia remembered the picture in the drawing-room and looked closely at it to see if the harpsichord already bore the black scar at the time when it was painted: but time had darkened the picture and obscured the details and it was impossible to tell. She mused over it for a time, wondering what her namesake had been playing so long ago.

She longed to know more about the dark figure in the background: was he perhaps a notable performer on the harpsichord? And what was it about him that so interested and baffled her?

She spent the rest of that day in the little panelled room, playing all the Mozart and Haydn sonatas she knew, and trying to put into practice what Mr. Bagenal had told her. She was entranced by the crisp, clear tone of the harpsichord, and the brilliant, sparkling sounds she was able to produce. It was all new and exciting to her, and yet somehow she had the feeling that she was coming back to an old friend, and that she and the harpsichord understood each other very well.

Uncle Frederic's voice broke the spell. 'This is delightful, Alicia – I had no idea you could play so well. You have indeed brought the old harpsichord to life again, and it is the greatest pleasure to hear it.'

When they came downstairs to Aunt Sophie in the drawing-room she said, 'Alicia dear, aren't you lonely up there? You have been playing for hours.'

'Lonely?' echoed Alicia. 'No, I feel at home in that little room, as if I had known it always, and not lonely in the least. I don't know why,' she added after a moment, looking a little puzzled, and her eyes strayed back to the picture as if seeking an explanation there.

The next morning was so glorious that Alicia went straight into the garden and stayed there till lunch-time, only wishing that Giles was there too, to enjoy the warm peaches off the wall and look with her at the natural history books she had found – he knew more about birds and butterflies than she did.

By the afternoon she could stay away from her little white room no longer. She knelt at the window for a time and looked at the garden from there; then for some reason she picked up the loose cushion on the window-seat and found that underneath was a hinged lid. This she lifted up and discovered a cupboard below it. Inside, a layer of fine dust covered piles of faded sheets of music.

They must have lain there undisturbed for a long time. Alicia held them close to the window and blew off the dust. 'I don't believe anyone has touched this music since the other Alicia put it away,' she said. 'This is the music she used to play. What funny old-fashioned titles. "*Nouvelles Suites de Pièces de Clavecin*", by Jean Philippe Rameau. "The famous 'Méthode' for the Clavecin or Harpsichord by François Couperin" – that looks rather heavy going. "Six Sonatas for the Harpsichord by Domenico Scarlatti" – Oh! I don't know where to begin!'

She propped the yellowish sheets of music before her and began to play, one piece after another – on and on she went. It was like a new world opening before her. She felt a mastery over the music which she had never had before. Her fingers were stronger and surer and she was filled by a sense of encouragement and sympathy.

Once or twice she had the strange feeling that she was doing again something she had done before, long, long ago. But it was only a fleeting impression, and was gone before she could pin it down. The interest of the music absorbed her beyond everything else.

What she could not account for was the comfortable sensation of having close by her a sympathetic listener, a friendly presence radiating encouragement and somehow imbuing her with powers she did not know she possessed.

But it was only puzzling when she thought about it afterwards – nothing could be more natural than this feeling of happy companionship and mutual understanding which possessed her again as soon as she sat at the harpsichord in her little white room the next afternoon.

Time slipped by and the shadows moved along the wall as she played on – dipping into all Alicia's music and rejoicing at her own unexpected prowess.

As the room grew darker she became increasingly aware of a figure which seemed strangely familiar listening intently in the shadowy corner. She was working away at a Pastorale of Scarlatti's now, playing it with enjoyment and feeling, though still imperfectly.

'You stumble at the old place, Alicia,' said a gentle half-humorous voice, which she felt she had always known.

'Yes – the old place,' she replied, 'but have patience with me and I will get it right.'

She tried again. 'Gently, child, don't hurry it – like this,' and he hummed the lovely phrase . . .

The lesson went on for a long time, till at last Uncle Frederic appeared at the door. 'Alicia, it is late and almost dark – Aunt Sophie sent me to fetch you. So odd – I thought I heard voices as I came along the passage. My imagination is leading me astray.'

Alicia looked wonderingly at him, rather as if she had been startled out of a dream. She was silent and preoccupied that evening, and sat gazing at the picture in the drawing-room as if trying to read there the answer to a riddle. Then she shook her head and laughed, kissed Aunt Sophie good-night, and cried, 'I've never been so happy! The days go too fast.'

Indeed, the days slipped by almost unnoticed, and when Alicia's mother rang up at breakfast-time one morning to say that Giles was as well as possible and they hoped to come and fetch her home the following day, she felt a pang of regret she could hardly conceal. With a face full of dismay she turned to Aunt Sophie. 'I'll be going home tomorrow! Giles hasn't got it – scarlet fever, I mean. Of course that's splendid – but I wish it didn't mean today is my last day.'

Aunt Sophie flushed with pleasure. 'That is very nice of you Alicia, and we shall miss you dreadfully. I only wish on your last day Uncle Frederic and I did not have to go out together – but it is such a long-standing promise . . .'

'Of course you must go. No, indeed I won't be lonely. I want a long last lesson on the harpsichord. I still have heaps to learn.'

It was a heavy, close afternoon with a hint of thunder, and the stillness was almost oppressive.

'It feels as if it's waiting for something to happen, it's so quiet,' said Alicia, and she waved to Aunt Sophie and Uncle Frederic from the steps as they drove away.

The garden was full of warm smells, but the birds were hushed and not a leaf was stirring. Alicia chose a ripe peach – 'My last.' She looked up at the house leaning above her, and waved towards the window of her little white room, then she turned and slowly climbed the familiar stairs.

'Here I am,' she said, and sat down as usual.

All through the long, still afternoon she played on and he listened. She did not see the darkening sky, nor hear the foreboding mutter of thunder – she was too intent to notice the sudden swirl of wind which rattled the open window and then died as suddenly.

As she turned the pages of her music she came on one she had not opened before– 'His Meditation', by Giles Farnaby. 'I've not played this for – how long?' whispered Alicia. But there was a great black scar right across the page. 'Just like the scar on the harpsichord: surely this was never here before? I can scarcely see the notes.' She bent close to make them out, and then clearly and sweetly the delicate phrases followed each other in ordered succession.

She played with the ease and surrender of long acquaintance, in the absolute stillness of an ominous hush. Then the mood of the music changed, and she faltered. 'Come, let me show you – I will play this for you,' he said, and he seated himself at the harpsichord in her place.

Alicia listened to the enchanted sounds, and marvelled at the magic of his playing.

Gradually as she listened she became possessed by the sensation which she had begun to feel once before, the realization that this had happened to her before, in some faraway half-remembered existence, and that she was powerless to prevent the catastrophe she knew was coming.

'Oh, come away,' she cried. 'Stop – stop playing! It's coming—'

There was a blinding flash and deafening roar of thunder.

Alicia lay still on the floor until Uncle Frederic and Aunt Sophie found her there and carried her downstairs.

She opened her eyes at last, and looked wonderingly at them for a moment, before she found her voice to ask what had happened.

'Oh, dear Alicia – don't try to talk yet, for a little while. We found you upstairs, unconscious, on the floor – the lightning must have come right in at the window. Drink a little water, now, and then smell this sal volatile, if you can. The music you had been playing was lying on the floor – it is a miracle you escaped as you did. We found you lying at a little distance away, not sitting at the harpsichord. But how do you feel, Alicia?'

'All right now, thank you, only I've a headache all over.'

said Alicia, and then she was silent and thoughtful for a long time.

Suddenly Aunt Sophie, who was watching her face, said, 'Frederic – the likeness to your grandmother's picture, it's quite uncanny – look!' Alicia was very pale, and it was partly this no doubt that made the resemblance between the two so startling.

'It might be you,' said Uncle Frederic in an almost scared voice. 'Sitting at your harpsichord.' Then he added, half playfully, 'But what about the crotchety old gentleman in the corner, Alicia? Is he as severe as he looks?'

Alicia sprang up and stood before the picture. 'Oh! you don't understand,' she cried. 'He plays wonderfully – you can't believe how beautifully he plays. And he isn't severe, he's – don't you see – he's *blind*! It was the lightning. That's why he looks so sad – that's what I could not make out about him. The lightning struck him as he was playing – it struck him instead of me.'

She broke off. Aunt Sophie looked very much alarmed – she put her hand to Alicia's forehead and said, 'Hush, dear, don't excite yourself. Don't talk any more now, just come quietly to bed – she must be quite delirious, Frederic.'

'Oh, you'll never understand,' cried Alicia, and with a sudden impulse she stretched up to the picture and kissed the pale hand at his side, and then the hand covering his eyes. 'No, they'll never understand,' she cried in despair. Then she allowed Aunt Sophie to lead her away to bed.

She was glad enough to lie down between the cool sheets and lay her head on the pillow. Just before she fell asleep she sat up and said aloud, 'I know what I'll do – I'll tell the whole thing to Mr. Bagenal. He will understand.'

The next morning she slept on and on and was only awakened by a vigorous fanfare on a motor-horn under her window.

'It's Giles – they've come to fetch me home,' she cried. She jumped out of bed and ran downstairs to find Aunt Sophie looking agitated in the midst of explanations to her mother. 'I've crept in several times this morning, and she's breathing quite regularly and has much more colour – but she's still asleep . . .'

'Hullo,' cried Giles, 'what's all this about you being struck by lightning? You lucky pig – nothing whatever has happened to me, and I've wasted ten days without you. Come on, pack up your bag, there's no time to be lost – the holidays are going to begin in earnest now.'

Giles swept her off – there was no time for a farewell visit to the harpsichord or the little white room, and she could barely glance at the picture on the drawing-room wall amid the flurry of thankyous and goodbyes before she was whirled away on the road for home.

THE DOLL NAMED SILVIO

by Michael Kernan

I HAD been at Cay Doge almost three weeks before I even heard about the Boones, and by then, of course, I'd met all the others. In fact Kathy introduced me to one family, the Reeserbees, on that first evening.

I remember thinking how curiously *grande-dame* of her, just a child after all, to stand like a statue there on the verandah in her full, ankle-length granny dress, hands clasped together before her, watching the limousine bring me down that long, slowly curving drive. It was as though she, and not her father, had engaged me as her companion (his word; I prefer governess), as though she herself had summoned me, commanded my presence in this remote, sickly, lush, jasmine-smelling hideaway on the coast of Florida. The road had been designed to reveal the house gradually, among the magnolia trees and the date palms and bougainvillea and palmettos and bamboos: a flash of ancient pink stone masked by Moorish filigree, a glimpse of a turret or two, a suggestion of Venetian balconies with mullioned windows separated by spiralling rococo columns, and then, suddenly, a final swooping curve and that incredible vista – the castle revealed: a Victorian millionaire's vision of paradise or, perhaps more accurately, a Renaissance scholar's rarebit nightmare.

It did, at that, exude a nightmare sense of foreboding, of those unspeakable intuitions no sooner formed by the dreamer than horribly confirmed in actual dream-event. Even the soft papery rustle of the palm fronds conveyed a certain whispering threat.

Her hair was long and mousy brown and gathered in the back by a dangling loose ribbon. Rather tall, she smiled vaguely down at me and murmured, coolly, 'Miss Coker?' while Jimmie the chauffeur stepped out and opened the door for me and fetched my two suitcases. (On the long drive out we had mainly discussed how and when my trunk would be picked up at the station.) She was still standing on the same spot on the glazed, worn tiles – worn down by generations of Spaniards, that is, certainly not by Floridians – when we shook hands, and then she motioned me ahead of her into the house. I would have guessed she was twelve if her father hadn't told me she was sixteen. I never was very good with children's ages.

It was only after I had marched ahead that I heard her turn and follow me: an odd scraping sound. I glanced quickly back. Already her hands were pulling the granny dress in an instinctive motion of concealment, but I had seen the heavy black shoe, the sole five inches thick.

Really, he might have warned me. I could appreciate his problem, having the girl's tutor take off without advance notice the very day he was sailing for Europe (I had been charmed with that, I must admit; I didn't realize anyone Sailed For Europe any more), but he might have told me that much. I had to get the rest of it from Jimmie. And of course Varna the cook, although I never could understand a word she said and didn't particularly care to.

In the beginning, Kathy was quite the little hostess at our solitary and rather grand dinner. She had ordered the red snapper *meunière* herself. For the occasion, she said. I had forgotten about Florida red snapper. Superb, with potato balls in parsley butter. Some sort of sweet, heavy, Southern vegetable, doubtless Varna's speciality, which I didn't touch.

After the first few remarks she subsided into a shy silence, speaking only when I asked her questions. It was to be our pattern from then on. I never did know exactly how it started or why. Yes, she enjoyed algebra and geometry, though sometimes she found them hard. No, she wasn't very happy with French. There were so many exceptions to the rules.

'And when you're not studying,' I said, 'what do you do? Play outside? Do you have friends here?'

'I don't go out much,' she said. 'Mostly I stay in the house.'

'But isn't it lonely? Out here so far from things?'

'Oh, I have my dolls.'

I was about to mention the tennis courts I had seen on the way in, overgrown but not irreparable, when I remembered the foot. So in some slight confusion I switched to swimming.

'Is there a good beach here?'

'I have two hundred and thirty-one,' she said. Her stare was so intense that I was quite taken aback.

'What?'

'Dolls,' she said. 'Would you like to meet some of them?'

In silence we took a little elevator, with filigreed Spanish ironwork, to the third storey. And here was an amazement: a playroom big enough to give a wedding reception in, but low-ceilinged and snug, with dormer windows and on three walls a marvellous signed mural by one of the great illustrators of the 'twenties, I forget his name, all billowing clouds and dream castles and girls on swings. Not my style at all, but really quite striking for what it was.

Without a word Kathy clumped to the far end, where at least a dozen large, cloth-faced dolls sat, flopped and drooped around a tea table.

'Miss Coker, the Reeserbees,' she announced. 'This is Mrs. Reeserbee—' She lifted a matronly figure from its chair, made it bow ever so slightly and cooed in a faint voice suggesting weariness, poverty and gentility, 'How d'you do?'

Then she did the same for Mr. Reeserbee (also quite worn, but portly and booming, with a scratchy alto voice; the workmanship was excellent, I should say Eastern European, perhaps Czech) and the larger children, Emily and Samuel and Lawrence and the twins Bert and Nancy, and on down the line. At one point a squabble arose between small Mildred and her even smaller brother William: much waving of arms and pushing of tiny chairs while Kathy rushed unobtrusively from one to the other, manipulating and jabbering in different child voices, until finally Mr. Reeserbee cleared his throat and rumbled, 'That will do, children, that will do,' whereupon the little ones giggled. A remarkable performance. I had a distinct sense, not only of each individual character, but of the family as a whole, a rollicking Micawberish image.

'But that's extrordinary,' I said. 'You have personalities for them all. And even different voices. Don't you ever get them confused?'

Kathy looked genuinely surprised. 'Oh no! How could I? They're all so different, you know. Sarah is the delicate one, she has asthma, and I don't think her heart is very strong. That's why she sits by her mother. And Lawrence—'

'But my dear, you have a real talent. I've never seen anything quite like it. I'm really impressed.'

She smiled slowly. 'You haven't seen the others.'

'You mean to say that all two hundred and—'

'Two hundred and thirty-one,' she nodded, trying to hide her pleasure with the diffident and secret and somehow disturbing little smile that I was to know so well.

Every evening over the next two weeks, following French and algebra, I had tea with them, learned to chat with them, to cluck over their children's illnesses, to laugh at their foibles, to draw them out about their astonishing complex histories. Really, it was the only time I could connect with the girl, the only time Kathy showed me anything of herself. I wasn't encouraged to touch them, however. I met the de Revenants, an elegant childless couple, three feet tall, in evening dress (he was a retired diplomat); the tiny Mipps family, six inches high with very squeaky voices and a propensity for losing one another; the great Vortigan clan, thirty of them, actors and mountebanks who affected the costumes of twenty different countries, travelled a lot and seemed to have a fairly sleazy background; the tragic, down-at-heel O'Briens, always in debt (he drank), always equally glum in the face of disaster or windfall; the very ordinary Smiths with their large infant daughter (half again as tall as either parent) plagued by bladder trouble; the suffocatingly rich Van Dubeens, three generations of them, who spoke only in effete gasps. And the singles, who might turn up alone but most often were invited to tea with one family or another: dashing, mustachioed Edward Dexter, former Civil War blockade runner; Sylvia Solvay, heiress to a bi-carbonate fortune and spoiled rotten; poor Gerhart Pfanstiehl, once the most brilliant high-wire performer in the world but now a splintered wooden wreck who went about on a stretcher too small for him, still wearing his spangled circus sash.

There were more. I simply can't remember them all. It was many days before I could organize our study schedule so that Kathy would have sufficient time to do her home-work properly. One entire wall of the playroom consisted of a closet with labelled drawers in which the dolls and their clothes were stored. The girl spent far too much time getting them in and out and dressing them. Such a precise child. She kept a mental calendar of all her families' appearances, each group being brought out like clockwork on an intricate schedule, some twice a week, some every five days, some weekly and so on.

One morning I was in the kitchen making sure Jimmie understood the shopping list I had given him (another amazement: I was expected to run the entire establishment as housekeeper, supervising gardener and steward), when Varna waddled in from the pantry, a sullen Aunt Jemima.

'Ah, there you are,' I said. 'We'll have veal birds tonight. Would you say two pounds of fillets are about right?'

'Ain't gone be dinner tonight,' she mumbled. 'You gone be alone.'

'I beg your pardon?'

As usual she looked past me. 'Miss Kathy won't eat down tonight.'

'I don't know why not. She's perfectly well.'

Varna sulked – I always wondered if she was dishonest – and shrugged in Jimmie's direction.

'It's the nineteenth,' he told me. 'She has her dinner by herself on the nineteenth.'

The two of them stood there, suspended in time, eyes fixed on nothing.

'For heaven's sake, why?' I turned to Jimmie. 'Why?'

'It's a special night. She has them dolls out.'

'But we've had the dolls every night.'

'Them other ones. The Boones.'

'But I've seen them all. Some more than once.'

'Not these. She don't bring these out but once a month. You know she likes everything just so.'

'And doesn't deign to come down to dinner? I hope you're not telling me that the child runs this house. Time someone took her in hand. She needs exercise. Out in the sun. She never talks to anyone but those everlasting dolls.'

'She don't talk much,' said Jimmie. 'That's for sure.'

'Nor does her father. Really, he could have told me more about all of this. Most inconvenient.' I meant inconsiderate.

'Well, Miss Coker,' Jimmie said slowly, settling himself on a ladderback kitchen chair with a cracked old leather drumhead seat, 'maybe there's a lot to tell and maybe there ain't.'

He motioned to another chair, but I preferred to stand. Then he talked.

Most of it I knew already, of course. About old man MacAdam, the grandfather, who had made a fortune in the Pennsylvania oil-fields, and another as a Standard Oil partner, and still another in Florida real-estate. And how he had left eight square miles of Florida jungle to his son Stanley, who had promptly turned it into Gran Venetia, Millionaire City, with a forty-foot plaster arch over the main entrance, twelve miles of canals, a footbridge modelled on the Ponte

Vecchio (slightly displaced), eighty blocks of streets, sidewalks and lamp foundations, three lagoons and, dominating it all, on a beautiful scimitar of white Atlantic sand beach, the castle Cay Doge, where Stanley and generations of future MacAdams were to spend their days amid putative *quattro cento* Italian confessionals, wall-sized Canaletto (school) paintings, crypto-Dürer sculptures of praying hands, whole rooms full of worm-eaten mahogany antique refectory furniture by Wilson Mizner, fountains from Seville, Padua, Vienna and Philadelphia, unbelievably dusty wall-hangings, early English Gothic fireplaces, twelve feet high, from Salisbury or possibly Cincinnati, saints' tombs allegedly stolen from Thuringian cathedrals, and the four-poster beds of obscure emperors, all ensconced between carved plaster ceilings and endless inlaid wooden parquet floors so dangerously slippery that green rubber runners had to be set down everywhere to form a hideous trail connecting all forty-six rooms. The very fraudulence of the castle gave it a peculiar menace: a feeling of things violated, of ancient secrets uprooted, of ghosts disturbed. Their mute rage filled the place.

Sometimes on an oppressively close afternoon, when even the lemon sun seemed weary of all that moist heat, I could sense a brooding, smouldering fury in the very trees and shrubs and vines that clustered around the buildings, choking it in airless gloom, their unceasing gentle clatter a whisper of conspirators.

I had been all over the estate by this time, and also had wandered past the crumbling Cay itself, where authentic gondolas were to have been moored – were, in fact, until the hurricane of '26, when they headed for Cuba in a group. It was the hurricane, of course, that scuttled Gran Venetia and other dreams.

Stanley MacAdam had been the man who hired me, and Kathy was his only daughter, for his wife (a society girl, no doubt, narrow-hipped and thin-blooded) had died giving birth. MacAdam rarely visited the place. Jimmie said he couldn't bear to see all those sidewalks sinking into the sand. It also pained him, Jimmie told me with unblinking glance, to see poor Kathy. The girl was to inherit forty-eight million exactly one year and a day after her eighteenth birthday, at which time Cay Doge was to become a state museum of some sort.

'You mean she'll have to leave,' I said.

He spread his palms before me. I simply can't stand the kind of man who makes gestures like that.

That afternoon, when the lessons were finished, Kathy complained she was feeling faint. Unthinkingly, I urged her to go to bed early, and it was only when I found myself taking dinner alone after correcting her papers that I remembered what Jimmie had said. I went up to her room on the second floor. She wasn't there, so I climbed the stairs to the playroom.

The door was locked. Voices came from the other side, the many voices in which Kathy could talk so freely, but harsh this time, angry and full of tension.

I knocked on the door, hard. 'I must come in,' I said. 'Kathy, let me in.'

After a full minute she opened the door and faced me with a sly smile. Her eyes flamed with something beyond hatred. She bowed me into the room.

Dolls of all sizes sat around on the floor. At least two dozen. There were no chairs or tea-tables. The dolls were humped stiffly forward or lay flat on their backs. They were unkempt, many in rags, some with the hair entirely gone and their bare pink pates shining dully in the soft light. Some of the skulls had been dented or smashed in the back. Then, as I looked from one doll to the next, all around that unlovely circle, I saw something else.

Every doll was blind. The cloth ones had ragged holes where the glass had been plucked clean out. The hard plastic ones with movable eyes all showed the whites. A few had nothing more than dark empty sockets.

'Kathy. What is this?'

'The Boones, Miss Coker.' Still that secret smile, the blazing eyes.

'But they're awful. You should throw them away.'

She stared with such frightening intensity that I diverted my glance to the dolls again. They seemed to confront me with accusations I could find no name for.

'Sort of a doll hospital, is that it? Where the sick ones come?'

She shook her head slowly.

'Well,' I said finally. 'Aren't they ugly. Do they talk? Perhaps you should talk to them.'

'They just talk to me,' she whispered, 'when there's no one around.'

'Well. If they're shy, perhaps we should do something about it. If you'd introduce me to them, I'm sure we—'

'They just talk to me,' she said, louder.

It was only then that I noticed the big one. It stood slightly back from the others in the gloom, dominating the circle with its outstretched arms. It must have been two feet high. An extraordinary figure, it appeared to be a Punch doll with fantastically hooked nose and jutting chin, pink gaiters, pointed floppy hat (like Father Christmas, I thought; no, rather more like Dante) and bulging eyes that had been painted black. Kathy saw me staring at it.

'That's Silvio,' she said. 'He's very old. He's the oldest of all.'

And slowly, watching me intently, she lifted the doll up to my face.

I saw at once it was no Punch. Malice glowed from its lacquered face, brown with age. The feet evidently had been sawn through at the base, doubtless by the thief or antiquarian who removed it from the great portal or crypt it once had adorned. It had to be Venetian, for surely that was a Doge's cap, I could see now. Yet the thing seemed far more ancient than any Renaissance carving. It was timeless.

While I gazed, shocked into silence, the blacked-out eyes – extinguished many centuries ago, I could guess from the dull cracked lacquer – hypnotized me. The arms, extended forward palm up as though they had once grasped a musical instrument, made me think of some horrid Chac-Mool holding out his obsidian platter to receive yet more bloody human hearts.

Of all the thousand stolen treasures in this spurious place, this doll alone was absolutely authentic. It wore its ingrained dustiness, its wormholes and chipped paint, its mutilated feet with the grandeur, the total arrogance of the real. And the grin, that curling grin, that leer of contempt and malevolence: what hatred must have gone into the making of this idol . . .

I backed out and said goodnight and left the child there with her terrible dolls. I didn't get to sleep for hours that night, I can tell you. Something sick was going on, and it was up to me to shake her out of it.

The next morning I announced immediately after breakfast that we would have our French recitation on the beach. Down to the sand with our books. The weather was conniving with me: it was a gorgeous day, clean and sunny and a touch of salt in the air.

'Come on,' I told her. 'Get your bathing-suit on, and I'll meet you in fifteen minutes.'

Response: zero. Really it was hard to talk to her. I changed in my room, thinking how curious that I, the teacher, should have to talk my young pupil into 'playing hookey', as it were. I may be heavy, but I am a strong swimmer, and I ached for an excuse to get into the lovely Florida water.

I needed my espadrilles for the long stroll down through the formal gardens, descending the coral steps to the sand. Just where the dunegrass ended I spread out the blanket, anchored it with the Larousse and the Erckmann-Chatrian we were reading and my ditty-bag and ventured into the water. It was cold. Bracing. A good word, bracing. I glanced back at the castle. And saw a remarkable sight.

Jimmie was coming down the steps. Carrying her in his

arms. She wore her eternal granny dress, which billowed in the breeze so that he had to feel his way with his feet. I couldn't help noticing that his arm under her thighs was bare.

'No bathing-suit?' I asked.

She smiled her irritating little smile.

'Oh come on. Here you are, with this glorious sun. You can get a tan. Don't you want a tan?'

Without a word he set her down on the blanket and, I might note, hustled back to the house.

'But you can walk perfectly well,' I said.

The girl was still smiling back at the retreating Jimmie. 'He wanted to,' she said. 'He likes to carry me sometimes for fun. Like he used to.'

I can't convey to you how she looked after him, that stumpy little figure with the sleeves rolled up over his hard-muscled arms, and jeans, and the bare brown neck that jutted above his collar. He was anywhere from twenty-five to forty, with yellow cat eyes that didn't tell you anything.

'Kathy, you must have a bathing-suit.'

She arranged the dress around her feet and stared dreamily out to sea.

'Tomorrow I want you to wear it. You do swim, don't you?'

She nodded in her reverie.

'We'll come here every day and swim. Wouldn't you like to swim. We can swim in French. It's "nager".'

She gave not the slightest sign that she understood my little attempt to be friendly.

'Heavens, a strong girl like you shouldn't need to be carried. You know, sometimes young men will try to touch you – well, it's not a good thing.'

Needless to say, the lesson didn't go well, and when the breeze started flipping the pages I gave up.

'That's enough for today, I think,' I said. But she wasn't listening; she was gazing out to sea, head oddly lowered, and her lips were moving while her hands fluttered about her pathetically undeveloped little bosom. I thought she was adjusting her dress, but then I noticed the head of a small doll poking up from her breast pocket. It was one of the Mipps dolls.

'Oh. You've brought a doll. I thought we had agreed the dolls wouldn't interfere with lessons.'

Wildly, she clasped her bosom and glared down at the offending tiny head. She pushed it out of sight with some violence and then, abruptly, swung herself to her feet and limped back up to the house, paying not the slightest attention to me, assuming as usual that people would pick up after her. As though she thought she was living in an hotel. (I told her as much once, and she merely did her turning-off act, her wan little face instantly going blank.)

A few days later, when we were having tea with the Mipps family, I noticed a certain strain; the children were sulky and hardly spoke, and the jolly parents seemed angry with them. Once the father shook his hand at them and would have waggled a finger if he could. 'You see what happens,' he grumbled in Kathy's lowest voice.

'What is it?' I asked.

'Oh,' muttered Kathy, setting the father down on his chair so viciously that his eyes rolled, 'Betsy got lost.'

'You shouldn't have taken her to the beach. Perhaps if you were to go down there yourself and look in the sand you might find her.'

She had barely been out of the house since that day but spent her free time lounging on the verandah and watching Jimmie in the garden. Arrange his work hours as I might, he always seemed to turn up where she was, his tanned, muscled torso glistening at her. Once I mentioned to him that his going without a shirt might offend her, but he simply turned his cat's gaze on me until my heart began to pound from nervousness and I had to look away.

Of course I forgot about Betsy Mipps. There was more than enough to keep my mind occupied without worrying about a missing doll. Perhaps if I had pursued the matter then and there I might have avoided what came later.

It was several weeks later, a Friday night. I remember that. Kathy had been in bed with a so-called summer cold for two days, miserably sniffling and sneezing in her room, occasionally napping but mostly just lying there with a far-away look. I brought up her dinner-tray (having neatly intercepted Jimmie on his way up the back stairs with it, thank you very much Jimmie) and offered to read to her from *The Mill on the Floss*, but she said she had just taken a pill and would sleep after eating.

When I returned an hour later the tray was outside her door. I was about to start downstairs with it when something made me feel I should look in on her. I opened the door a crack. She was gone, the bedclothes flung back with great energy.

Hurrying up to the playroom, I tried the knob silently. It was locked, of course, but by this time I had located a duplicate key, hung on a great dusty board bristling with hooks and labels that I had found in a closed-off butler's pantry.

There were voices. I put my ear to the door.

'No! Please!' A tiny, squeaking cry.

'It is ordered.' Stern, magisterial.

'I won't do it ever again! I swear!'

'It has been decided.'

'But I couldn't help it. Oh, please!'

A rustling. Mutterings. The high whimpering of a terrified child. 'She is prepared.' A rasping alto voice.

A long silence, broken only by muffled keening. Then a sharp cry.

I rushed into the room.

The Boones sat in a tight circle around Kathy. Close to her almost head to head as though conspiring with her hulked the dark figure of Silvio. In the dim light she was bending over a piece of two-by-four upon which was tied a small doll.

Kathy jumped up. She had an old-fashioned buttonhook with a beautifully incised silver handle. There was nothing

in her face at all, only a strange calm, triumphant and quite mad.

I glanced at the doll. It was the Betsy Mipps doll. Its eyes had been pulled out.

Kathy smiled at me with a queer condescension, and her face softened. 'It's the nineteenth,' she said.

I think I screamed. I ran out of the room and down the stairs. Jimmie and Varna met me on the mezzanine.

'Get her out of there!' I shouted. 'Get those dolls out of there!'

They both ran on up, while I clung to the bannister. After a few minutes Jimmie came down, and I confess I more or less collapsed on him so that he had to support me down the stairs into the big study, where he helped me into an old Spanish leather chair studded with large brass knobs, rather like an electric chair, I remember thinking.

'Why, she's out of her mind,' I told him. 'She's gone out of her mind over those horrible dolls. We've got to do something!'

'It's okay now. Take it easy. Varna's getting her back to bed.'

'But we've got to get her away from them. Did you see what she—'

Jimmie was patting my forearm. His hand was warm and solid. 'She's just playing,' he mumbled. 'Kids play rough sometimes. It's okay.'

'You mean to say she's done this before? Well. I'm calling Dr. Porter in the morning. About a psychiatrist.'

'Now you just take it easy, Miss Coker. She don't feel good, with that cold.'

'I certainly will not take it easy. The girl is mentally ill. She needs attention, and right away. She shouldn't be allowed— Did you see those others? And that Silvio—'

He backed off and covertly eyed the stairs. 'Oh now. I don't think she did all them. They broke when she was playin' with 'em. They're awful old, some of 'em. Some of 'em even b'longed to her mother.'

'Nonsense! This is serious! She may have to be hospitalized.'

He grunted disapproval.

'I'm calling Dr. Porter in the morning. And if he thinks we should call in a specialist, then I'll cable Mr. MacAdam. He should absolutely know right away.'

Jimmie seemed relieved. 'Yeah, we should ask Mr. MacAdam. Maybe he'll fly back.'

'Maybe so.' I stood up, still slightly dizzy from sudden exertion and shock. 'But what I can do right now is lock those dolls up. I want you to change the lock on that playroom.'

'Oh now.'

'Don't talk back to me! I'm in charge of this house! I want that lock changed tonight!'

He shuffled and glared at me with his yellow eyes.

'Don't b'lieve I got 'nother lock around—'

'Well, you'll drive into town and pick one up. Or take one off the old boathouse door. You'll manage, I know.'

'Miss Coker—'

'Tonight! It's important for the girl's health.'

He lumbered off, shoulders hunched with rage. Later that night I heard him bumping about overhead, dropping things and cursing. Really, such a transparent little man. In any case, there was a shiny new Yale lock on the door when I checked next morning before breakfast. I saw him in the kitchen after, still not looking me in the eye, and I should have asked him for the keys then and there.

Most of the day I spent waiting for Dr. Porter to return my call. His office finally discovered that he was off for the day – Florida efficiency! Of course I could hardly be expected to deal with the junior partner, who wouldn't know the girl's background. In the evening I took a solitary swim, strolled in the gardens and read. Anything to stay out of that stifling house. Wherever I went the palm fronds clacked and rustled in the jasmined air.

After dinner Varna came down with the tray and the

message that Miss Kathy wanted to see me and explain.

'There's nothing to explain,' I replied.

'She want to see you,' the woman repeated in her dogged, sullen way. 'She call through the door. She in the playroom.'

'The playroom!'

I was so furious I ran all the way. I could have killed Jimmie. The door was unlocked. I yanked it open and stamped in. A shout of anger was on my lips.

It was like walking onstage. I was in the centre, and all around were dolls. On tables and chairs, on the floor, sitting and standing against the wall. All in a great ring. Ranged in tiers as though in an amphitheatre. Hundreds of them. All facing me. Huge cloth-faced ones, small china ones, girl dolls, baby dolls, adult dolls. All in a circle around me, staring at me. And in the centre, in the front row, sat the hideous Boone family. The limp, small figure that had been Betsy Mipps was one of them, her black eyeholes glaring at me like the rest.

In the very middle stood Silvio. The ringmaster. His angular face with its fixed, curving leer seemed to radiate an obscene delight, as though he were gloating over some delectable revenge upon this place and everyone in it. Across his outstretched hands lay the silver buttonhook.

I was aware that my mouth hung open. The scream wouldn't come.

A white flash. The back of my head seemed to explode. Then it was black.

The next thing was waking up in the pitch dark and hearing someone gasp and retch. And a man's voice saying over and over, 'Oh my God. Oh my God.' Then a woman: 'Quick, get her head up. Her face. The blood . . .'

I remember wondering how they could possibly see anything in such a velvety darkness, and then I fainted.

By the time I came out of the hospital Mr. MacAdam had long since returned from Europe and had arranged a very generous settlement for me. Poor man, he was shattered. His voice cracked, and his hands shook. Oddly enough, he was more upset about my condition than about Kathy, who will be in the other hospital for the rest of her life, I presume. I visit her sometimes. I'd like to visit her more often, but it's hard for me to get around by myself still. And anyway, she'll only consent to see me on the nineteenth of each month.

SUMMER SHADES

by Oliver Knox

THE programme page of the *Cork Examiner* for July 31st, 1974, gives 6.45 p.m. for the start of *The Archers*. I've even checked that time with Radio Four, and yes, that was when *The Archers* was broadcast. So I didn't imagine anything. I'm not mad. I'm not even bad!

But I had better begin at the beginning. Ever since I was twelve (and I am now eighteen) I used to feel a little left out of things during our summer holidays on the coast of West Cork. This wasn't just because my parents often left me to fend for myself, while they sailed away in their yacht, or because our cottage stands alone on a windy promontory. No, *that* solitude and wilderness I used to find romantic, used to hug to myself. The real reason, which it still hurts me to confess, is that I was never wholly accepted by the people in the next bay, even though our families knew each other quite well in London, and I was at school with one of the boys. After what has happened I can't speak ill of any of them; and in any case, they didn't even form a gang or anything, they weren't even standoffish. It was simply that Tim, Matthew, Oliver, Lucy and the rest never made me feel that I was quite one of them, or I could go in and out of their summer cottages as easily as they could with each others'.

Many afternoons I would scramble up to the rocky hilltop which separated our promontory from their bay and stand gazing down and wonder whether I should be welcomed in their settlement; or whether I should not be happier returning to our tiny shingle beach, to launch my dinghy and sail out alone round the islands.

But there were one or two occasions every summer when I would be invited to join forces with them. There was the Great Picnic on Horse Island, there was the night spent in the island hut, where a dozen of us from the ages of – oh, ten to nineteen – would huddle in our sleeping-bags and tell stories and be woken by horses sniffing and snorting round the walls; and, best of all there was the evening in the Haunted House. Over the years, these expeditions became a set part of the holiday calendar, and at least I was always included in them, *except* this last summer.

Five minutes' walk from the next farmhouse, down a 'green road' brings one to the haunted house. No one, not even the local shopkeeper, seems to know who owns it nowadays. They say that five winters ago a 'foreign lady' wearing a long mink coat descended in a hired car, and bought it from a farmer who has since died. At any rate, she left instructions that the windows should be boarded up, and the doors bolted and barred. Which was done, except that the board has fallen out of one of the windows, and someone forgot to attend to the back door, so that it can easily be pushed open or shut on the single hinge which is left, thin with rust.

But the property which I liked best is the walled orchard of apple trees – or perhaps I should say the orchard that long ago was walled, the trees that long ago bore apples. On wet days a rotting odour rises from the marshy earth; and, for many years on the last afternoon of the holidays I would pay a solitary visit and relish the bittersweet indulgence of sitting moodily on one of the fallen trunks (which still seem to sprout a few shoots, refusing to die altogether). I don't suppose I shall ever do that again now.

I never liked to admit as much even to myself: but I did not find the actual house, tumbledown and picturesque though it is, to be very 'ghostly', so I don't know how it came by its name. I don't count the one slight mystery, which was this: I never saw anyone come near it other than the summer families, yet whenever I went there, and peered through the window, I saw the glass on the rickety kitchen table had one or two wild flowers freshly put in it – a few pimpernels or dog-roses or something.

This glass we always said belonged to the house, and it is the one we first used for planchette two summers ago, on the best Haunted-House Party of all, when the girls came dressed-up as witches in long tattered robes and black shawls over their heads. Whether anyone cheated or not, the planchette was a great success: Tom (who would have been nineteen this month) had planed and polished the table the day before, and Dora had traced and cut out a huge Gothic alphabet. The letters and the empty tin of Johnson's wax were still in the fireplace last summer – probably are still there today.

I think it was all the dressing-up that evening which gave me the idea for a practical joke a day or two afterwards. One of the local farmers is a very good-natured man, always taking visitors out in his fishing boat, giving children rides in his donkey-cart and so on. He has an enormous strawberry-plot, and right in the middle of it, a very realistic scarecrow complete with a deerstalker hat and long shabby fawn mackintosh. When I asked to borrow it for a day, he just said, 'Good luck to you then.' He didn't bother even to ask me what I wanted it for.

It was a Saturday and the grown-ups were throwing a big barbecue for all the bay at Christopher's house. I wasn't invited, but there was no reason why I should have been. My parents were still away on their yacht. At about two o'clock I took out my dinghy, stowed the scarecrow, and sailed round very quietly to a little cove just underneath one of the other houses. I was pretty sure it would be empty and unlocked and so it was. Then I sat the scarecrow down by the fire, sat a glass of Guinness by his side and put a toy pistol by his hand. From outside the window at least, it looked quite convincing. Then I charged across the field to

Christopher's house, shouting, 'There's a stranger in Oliver's house! A stranger! I don't know who he is! He's got a gun in his hand! A gunman!! Help!'

Naturally there was a fair shemozzle. It didn't take long to sort things out and one or two people (I think they had had rather a lot to drink) even managed a faint laugh. Still the joke fell pretty flat, and though no one said anything much to me directly, I know that the parents thought it to be in poor taste, and it was probably why I found myself more than usually excluded that summer.

In fact, I wasn't even invited to the famous Haunted-House Party. I knew very well it was to take place because I overheard Oliver and Lucy discussing arrangements in the village shop. When they saw me Lucy nudged Oliver and they both fell silent. This made me feel very moody and upset – the sort of moodiness that leads to my kicking stones as I walk – and I tried to think of some revenge or action of *some* sort, *any* sort, all that day. Invited or not, *I would go.* I would dress up as the most horrific ghost or spook anyone had ever seen and give them all as much fright as I possibly could. I hoped they would be really terrified. I hoped they would *scream.* They couldn't even say anything afterwards, in the way they had scorned my previous year's scarecrow. After all, if you go to a haunted house surely you want it to be haunted. So my motives were thoroughly mixed, one part of me wanting to scare them out of their minds, the other part to impress them so much that I would be welcome back into the circle afterwards as a reward.

I would be thorough. I made a list of all the things I needed, and ticked all those which I needed to buy:

TOMATO JUICE✓
SELLOTAPE✓
SOOT
FLOUR✓
CARDBOARD
STRING

RAM'S HORN
SHEET
WHISTLE

I asked the shopkeeper's wife, Betty, whether there was any difference in colour between the two brands of tomato juice she had on her shelves. 'I'm sure I don't think it makes a ha'porth of difference to the taste,' she said. 'Isn't it Worcester sauce they sometimes put into it?' 'I don't mind about the taste,' I said; but it gave me an idea, and I bought some Worcester sauce too. 'I want it to look like blood,' I said. She shook her head at me, not understanding.

Soot was simple, and I soon dislodged a good pile of black peat-soot from the chimney on to pages of the *Cork Examiner*, without making too much mess. Our linen cupboard isn't very well stocked, but one double sheet looked older and thinner than the other two.

That left the ram's horn which I intended to fix on to my head. There's a small promontory near our own cottage; it gives just enough pasturage to tempt sheep on to it, and I'd seen the skeleton of a ram there one of the first days of the holiday. I hoped it wouldn't be too smelly, then rebuked myself for half-heartedness. Taking our biggest kitchen-knife, I set off brushing through gorse bushes and scrambling under barbed-wire. The skeleton was still there, a peregrine falcon hovering overhead. It wasn't easy separating the skull from the rest of the body, and I felt triumphant when I managed it at last, panting like a huntsman who's just caught his prey.

By six-thirty on the evening of the party, I had assembled all my ghostly baggage. It was blowing a near-gale and I bent my head into the wind and clutched hard at the ram's horn and the sheet, as I walked across the paddock to the lee of the hedge where I kept my fourth-hand Volkswagen. My face was already smeared with the mixture of tomato juice and flour, and two small trickles of Worcester sauce dripped from my mouth. No doubt I was a terrible 'sight', and would have felt ridiculous if my feeling of rejection had not been urging me on.

Judging from the previous years, the others would by now have arrived at the haunted house. Still I must avoid at all costs any risk of running into them, so I took a very roundabout way by tiny back lanes. The only place of danger was the old iron bridge which spans the neck of the estuary, past the village.

I'm always frightened going over the bridge. I'd guess it's at least two hundred yards long. It's very narrow, barely enough for the width of a single car. The iron legs and the railings both seem very rusty, and the surface of the road is full of cracks. There are threatening notices about no vehicles over so many tons. Often the wind funnels down the estuary and feels as if it were lifting the car up, so it's definitely *not* the place to break down.

Which, of course, is exactly what happened that evening. The old Volkswagen gave a few 'phut phuts' and stopped dead in the middle of the bridge. I got out and began to tinker. My eyes smarted with the wind and irritation. After a few minutes I ran my fingers through my hair (remembering just in time *not* to rub my hand over my smeared face), and wondered what to do next. Something which looked like a breakdown lorry drove slowly down the road which intersected with the far end of the bridge. I shouted and waved at it. No luck.

Then I noticed my transistor radio in the back seat – well, what *used* to be the back seat – of the car. Some music might soothe me, even suggest some solution to my mechanical problems. I tuned into the VHF station. It was the end of the programme. I even remember clicking my fingers at the sound of 'Barwick Green'. I tightened up a few more bolts in a hopeless way, and more from want of anything else to do than in serious expectation I tried the started once again. Miracle. I coaxed the engine back into stuttering life, and turned off the radio just as the time-pips pipped seven o'clock. I hadn't wasted more than twenty minutes at the most. I wouldn't be late. And I couldn't have been spotted.

To reach the haunted house, you can turn either left or right after crossing the bridge, before striking inland half a mile up (or down) the coast road. There seemed to be some commotion to the right, probably to do with the breakdown lorry I had seen. There was no point in getting mixed up with *that*, so I turned left, and patted the steering-wheel, pleased with my change of luck.

I parked in the lee of a fuchsia hedge, in an old ditch of a lane on the further side of the house – not the direction from which we usually approached it. Then, feeling foolish for the first time, and almost regretting the escapade, I put on my sheet and fitted the ram's horn contrivance over my head. I couldn't help the sinking feeling that I wasn't going to fool anyone, and nearly gave up and went home. If only I had! Though what difference would it have made?

The way to the house from this side is very boggy and several times I was up to my ankles in mud. I was wearing plimsolls and I loathe getting my feet wet. The wind tugged at the ram's horn, turning it askew. I scrambled over some barbed wire and ripped the sheet. But once I had climbed over the broken wall of the orchard, my heart began to pound a little faster and I persuaded myself I would make a very good spook after all.

Flattening my back against the wall, like a criminal in a film. I edged the last few yards towards the window of the room where I knew they would all be assembled. Yes! Eight of them on the floor in a circle. And a blackened saucepan on the fire, which was smoking horribly, as it always did. None of them were dressed up at all. James was rolling back and waving, so that he lay almost full-length staring up at the plasterless ceiling. Christopher and Tim were playing some sort of card-game, Tim cupping his chin in the palm of his hand, Lucy and Oliver were holding hands, and I felt a pang of jealousy. Lucy was the girl I would have liked to kiss, but never dared say so. Obviously the party was just beginning.

Edging back again I broke off a twig from one of the apple-trees, returned and began to scrape the window. That might make them look round. I continued to scrape for a couple of minutes, taking care to keep well out of sight. Then I lifted the sheet, felt in my pocket, took out the whistle, and played a few bars of 'Three Blind Mice' and stopped. Perhaps that was an unsuitable choice, not ghostly enough. I should have practised earlier in the day. An Irish ghost would surely play Irish tunes? 'Sweet Molly Malone' was the only one I could think of. I played it very slowly indeed and cautiously peeped into the window.

The wind had dropped – although the boughs of the apple-trees still rustled – the sky had blackened, and one or two heavy drops of rain had just begun to fall. At the very moment that I stopped in front of the window a flash of lightning lit up the dirty panes of glass and everyone in the room looked round simultaneously I bowed my ram's horn head up and down three times gravely, and slid away from the window. A distant roll of thunder. The drops of rain were now becoming heavier, and a downpour threatened. No matter. I was exultant. I walked across the window boldly so that I could be seen in profile, whistle to my mouth. I didn't mind being recognized now, so well had my plan already succeeded. At the other side of the window I jumped happily in the air, then saw an opportunity for a further stroke. One of the old trees was dead and rotten, only just standing. Its roots had quite recently been half-torn from the ground, perhaps by the gale earlier that very day. Energetic shoving might push it right over. I leant against its trunk with my bottom and heaved as mightily as I could. I felt the slow wrench of roots and the tree laboriously descended. A second later, more lightning, closer thunder. One or two more panes seemed broken now. The effect now was far more melodramatic than anything I had dared hope. I clambered round the fallen branches and looked full into the window, raising my arms out, and splaying my legs as if in a physical exercise. I tried to gibber, opened and shut my mouth, nodded my ram's horn head.

I stopped my antics to draw breath. I could not have been more delighted by the sight that met my eyes. All the group were now huddled in a corner at the far side of the room. Oliver was hugging Lucy, her face buried in his chest. Jamie, it's true, was more debonair, pointing commandingly towards the window, but even he stood pressed back against the wall. Christopher had his forearm over his brow as though to shield himself from whatever might come next. Tim was kneeling on the floor. He looked as if he were praying, however unlikely that may seem to those who used to know him.

One very peculiar thing – but one which struck me with force only when recalling the affair later – was how wet everyone appeared to be. No, not just wet; they were soaked to the skin, clothes clinging to their bodies. Yet it had not been raining for more than five minutes at the most, and in any case they were all sitting *inside*. Certainly the ceiling has lost all its plaster, but there is another room above, and the roof is still slated. So there was no need to get soaked at all. But at the time I was getting so wet myself that I didn't pay much attention to this.

The hem of the sopping sheet was chafing my wrist, water was running down my neck. It was time to bring my joke to its climax. Surely they couldn't fail to agree that this time I had scored a complete triumph! With a long melancholy wail I kicked open the door and, waving my arms, my face dripping with tomato juice and rain, stumbled into the room.

Amazement! This was ridiculous, fantastic! So thoroughly had I scared them that they were scrambling out of the window, Tim in the rear jumping clean over the window-sill in panic. Half out of breath with my wailing and charging around, I leant out of the window and gazed after them. They were streaking down the green road at astonishing speed, crowded together in a pack. I didn't feel up to chasing them, they had got too well away. Instead I contented myself by shouting 'LEMMINGS' after them. Lemmings makes a good yell because of that double-m. LEMMINGS! LEM-M-INGS!

By now they had probably reached their old Dormobile. Then I felt a bit let down. I took off my ram's horn and my sopping sheet and wandered round the room. I ate two of the blackened sausages left in the frying-pan. They were cold and tasted very stale. I wished I had brought the remainder of the Worcester sauce with me. I put a few sticks on the fire to warm myself up a bit. I would wait until the rain had stopped.

Being alone in the house, with all the cobwebs and damp and diet, wasn't very pleasant. I shivered. Would I catch a cold? And how silent the house felt – which reminded me how strangely and *silently* the others had fled, no hooting with laughter, no screaming in panic, real or pretended. The patter of the rain outside seemed to add to the silence inside. I jumped when I heard a scratching noise, and was relieved when I looked round and saw a mouse scamper along the wainscot.

Now the house seemed really haunted – a sort of emptiness flowing in and out of the room – I can't describe it. To hell with the rain, I'd clear out. I fixed the ram's horn to one of the rafters with a bit of old wire, to preside over the memory of the occasion; and wiped my face thoroughly with the wet sheet to remove the tomato juice and Worcester sauce. (That felt horrid.)

Driving home, I recovered my spirits, and even laughed out loud as I speeded downhill at 50 m.p.h., the most that my Volkswagen can do. I confess to some mixture of bitterness in my laughing, because I would have much preferred to have enjoyed my success with the others. Their flight still left me *out* of it. Still, better to have triumphed on one's own than not at all.

There were a lot of Garda about and I was glad I had cleaned myself up. I know it's not criminal to drive about with a face looking as if covered in blood, but I didn't want to stop for questioning.

I didn't feel in the least hungry when I got home. I'd smoke a cigarette and go to bed. Just as I was going upstairs I noticed, scrumpled beneath the door, a note which I opened and read. 'HAUNTED HOUSE TONITE 6PM DO COME LOVE LUCE.'

So I need never have bothered with all that charade! How foolish I felt – but above all pleased and happy, *absurdly* happy and relieved that I wasn't an outcast after all! No bed now – I would drive over to the bay and join the gang immediately, and wallow in the glory of my exploit. They must have got over their fright by now, if indeed it ever *was* fright.

(But when had the note been left? Had it been there all morning and I'd never seen it? Alas, that's one minor puzzle I'll never solve now.)

When I drove back to the bay and knocked at the door of Christopher's house no one answered. And the same at Tim's house. No grown-ups or children to be seen anywhere. Perhaps they had gone for some late-evening expedition – the sunset was very fine after all the rain. I left Lucy's house till last, out of shyness. Her mother opened the door:

'Is Lucy in . . .?' I began.

She just turned and ran back into the house. I heard her cry, 'Peter, do come. Come *now*. Paul's here.'

I called out after her, 'It doesn't matter. I mean I hope I'm not interrupting or anything.'

There was silence. I went on, 'I couldn't help coming now. You see we had such a super joke. I'm sorry, though . . .'

Lucy's father came out, looking dreadfully yellow and stern. He said, 'There's nothing we can do. Nothing anyone can do.'

I didn't follow him at all, and said, 'But we had great fun really, apart from the storm and getting wet. That's what I came about – the joke. And to thank Lucy, for asking . . .'

'Come in,' said Lucy's father, and shut the door behind me.

'You obviously haven't heard.'

'Heard what?'

'Oh, God!'

My stomach dropped. Lucy's father went on, speaking carefully.

'Of course you haven't heard. Forgive me.'

He left me and came back again with two glasses of whisky. He said, 'The whole lot of them were in the Dormobile. The whole lot, all of them. We've just come back. There was nothing we could do.'

I could hear his wife moving about in the next room. He said, 'Look, I'd better tell you. The van went off the road half a mile from the bridge. It seems . . .' He broke off.

'Look, Sir,' I said. 'I'm afraid I don't know *anything*.'

'Of course not. Why should you? There's no hope. Absolutely no hope at all. They've recovered six of the . . . bodies. So far. That's all there is to say.' He wasn't even drinking his whisky. He added, blankly, 'What did you say about a joke?'

I told him agitatedly how I played ghost, and the others had 'pretended' to be frightened. He didn't seem to be listening. I gulped my whisky.

'Ah well,' he said, and got up, and let me out.

Outside the door I stamped my feet. I wondered if I could trust myself to drive back. In the end, I got home, and slept much better than I had expected – shock I suppose – and only when I woke up early next morning did I gradually thaw: the realization of what I had done flooded in on me. *I* had killed them. I had frightened them literally out of their wits. I closed my eyes tighter and tighter till I could see a purple ball of fire. If I could grasp, become part of, the whole horror here and now, it would be better. Only after *seeing* it all, *seeing* the gang pelt down the green road, pile into the Dormobile, tear round the bend . . . only after all that could I begin to imagine what life would be like in the future, how it would feel to be a murderer. I deliberately called myself a murderer. I wasn't going to let myself off.

I never get up early when my parents are away. That morning I lay in bed even later than usual, staring at the ceiling, only my head out of the blankets. I don't know when it was I heard loud knocks, came downstairs in my pyjamas, and opened the door to a Garda. He had a white face, and blue eyes that didn't look at me.

'It's a terrible tragedy, altogether,' he said. 'They're saying you were the last one to see them alive.'

I said, 'But that was at the house with the orchard near Driscoll's farm. Miles away from where . . .' I began to feel even more of a murderer.

'Ah,' he said, 'we're just checking around. How were they seeming when you saw them last?'

'Well, we used to call it the haunted house and have parties there. I was playing ghost. They all pretended to be frightened and ran away down the road – I went home in my own car.'

'Ah, sure, that was it,' said the Garda. 'Nothing unusual about the way they behaved?'

'No – well nothing *I* saw,' I lied. He stood for a while leaning against the door and eyeing me.

'It doesn't sound an advisable carry-on, at all at all,' he said. I didn't reply. 'Well, I must be going along. If there's nothing more you can tell us.'

I was shaking with fear by the time he left. I wondered who had told him about my 'joke' – it must have been Lucy's father. I was mad with guilt and anguish and didn't leave the house all day. I hoped no one would ever see me again. I would become a hermit.

And two whole days really did pass before I moved more than a hundred yards from our cottage. I lived on baked beans and stale bread. On the third day I saw my parents' yacht sail back through the channel, and anchor between the island and our promontory. They had cut their holiday short when they had heard the news, thinking they must return if they could possibly be of help: at the very least to attend the funeral.

On the kitchen table they left the copy of the *Cork Examiner* which had brought them the news. I read:

7 DROWNED IN COAST ROAD DISASTER

A Dormobile van belonging to an English holiday-maker left the road near —— last night, breaking through the wall and falling into the sea. Seven children between 12 and 18 years of age lost their lives. The cause of the tragedy is being investigated. No one was present at the accident scene, but the alarm was given by Fr. Doyle at 6.30 and by 7.30 the first five of the bodies had been recovered from the sea.

Only at the second reading of the story did I notice the times.

But at seven o'clock I was on the bridge, on my way to the haunted house! I couldn't be – wasn't – mistaken. That was something I *knew*.

Then other memories rushed into my head. I remembered the breakdown lorry I'd seen when I was tinkering with my car on the bridge. I remembered the soaked figures in the haunted house. I remembered the strange way they had all fled silently, in a pack. I remembered the Garda on the road on my way home.

And then – well, later as I said I checked the times of the programmes for July 31st. *The Archers was* the programme I had heard on the bridge. 6.45 p.m. *was* the time it was transmitted

And that's all there is to it. But whatever on earth – or not on earth – did I see that evening? What exactly *did* I scare? What summer shades? Will they ever come back?

NICOLA

by D. A. Koster

THE almost irresistible desire to visit the Tremiti Islands really became a conscious factor in my thoughts more than twenty years ago, although – like many adolescent passions which diminish as one grows up – I then forgot the place completely as the day-to-day business of earning my bread and butter became an all-consuming occupation.

I remember reading, somewhere, that most people are so busy with living that they have no time to live, and that was certainly true, at that time, in my own case. Because of those thoughts, it was perhaps somewhat ironical that my youthful dream became a reality, so many years later, only by the benevolence of a long-forgotten uncle. He had gone to New Zealand as a young man and so devoted himself to the business of living that, by the time he died, he had gathered enough of the world's wealth to leave me, his only surviving nephew, enough money to enable me to dispense entirely with that same business of living for the rest of my life – if I was fairly careful.

But I decided not to be too careful – and so I went, at long last, to the Tremiti Islands.

It all began when I was about sixteen. My father kept a bookshop in Charing Cross Road and in those days, when I was trying – but without much enthusiasm – to become a solicitor's clerk, I used to lunch at a small Italian restaurant in Soho, where I became friendly with the proprietor's daughter who used to serve at table when they were busy. One day, when I was lunching late and the restaurant was almost empty, she told me how, after her mother's death, her father had brought her to England from their native Italy and first worked as a waiter himself in that same restaurant.

She spoke English fluently and conversed in a charming easy manner, and remembered enough of her childhood years to convey such a magical picture of the island where she had been born that my own grey humdrum life in London seemed a nightmare by comparison. I suppose it must have added to the romance of the occasion when she told me that her name, Nicola, was the same as that of her birthplace.

A few months later, browsing through a new batch of travel-books in my father's shop – my chief leisure occupation at that time – I came across one entitled *Both Sides of the Adriatic*. On the front cover there was a colour picture of a tiny island floating on an azure sea and peeping through a gap in some trees. On the flyleaf I read: 'Cover picture: Isola San Nicola di Tremiti, from Isola San Domino.' Could this possibly be, I wondered, Nicola's own island?

Next day I took the book to the restaurant, and that evening, sitting with me at a corner table in the quiet hour or so before the invasion of diners, she was wafted back on a magic carpet to her island home, for so it proved to be – and she took me with her. The island was, indeed, Saint Nicola, one of the Tremiti Islands off the east coast of Italy.

I really think I must have fallen a little in love with Nicola that evening, for we saw a lot of each other after that. But when, about a year later, my firm of solicitors moved to the north of England and I went with them, Nicola's letters became less and less frequent as she mentioned with increasing regularity her friend Antonio, and soon she was no more than a very dear memory.

Nearly twenty years later and soon after my uncle's death, when I became financially independent for the first time in my life, I had a letter from a friend of mine who had gone to Italy after the war and had done very well for himself. He had heard of my good fortune through a mutual acquaintance, and wrote to me from Naples.

'If you are giving up your job,' he said, 'as I imagine you will be, why not come out here and spend the summer with me? A few years ago I acquired a converted off-shore fishing boat. I have six months' accrued holiday to take and I am thinking of going up the Adriatic – along the Yugoslav coast – and perhaps as far north as Venice. I should be glad of your company and of your assistance.'

So it came about, early in May, that I joined him in Naples and we set off. It was his longest, and my first cruise in the Mediterranean. We were both terribly excited.

A couple of days later we left Syracuse on the east coast of Sicily for Budva in Yugoslavia, three hundred and sixty miles away. Eastwards, under the toe of Italy, then across the Gulf of Taranto to the heel – blessed, surely by the angels, with the delightful name of Capo Santa Maria di Leuca. The following week, with a picture-postcard sea and sky of brilliant blue for our hundred-and-fifty-mile crossing of the southern end of the Adriatic, we arrived at Budva – a fascinating little walled town nestling behind the four-hundred-feet-high Oticic Sveti Nikola.

More than two months after that, when I landed on that other island, Isola San Nicola, at the beginning of what were destined to be the happiest years of my life, I wondered why this first Islet of Saint Nikola at Budva had not stirred my memory. Thinking back now, I suppose it did – for I remember having, at the time, a queer half-conscious feeling that I ought to be remembering someone, or something else.

It was before we left Venice towards the end of August, and while studying the charts of the east coast of Italy to decide where to stop for a day or two, that I noticed a group of four small islands about twelve miles off-shore and just north of that mountainous spur, the Promontorio del Gargano, which projects from the leg of Italy about a hundred and fifty miles up the coast from the heel. They were the Isole Tremiti.

I pored spellbound over the chart – at Caprara, San Domino, Il Cretaccio . . . and at San Nicola. Twenty years vanished like a flash. I was back in that little Soho restaurant talking to Nicola – and I knew at once that I had to go to the islands.

They were almost on our direct route back and I had no trouble in persuading John that there was nothing else nearly as interesting anywhere along the Italian coast. I wanted to arrive very early in the morning, at first light if possible, so as to be sure of spending at least one whole day there. If the weather broke we should have to run for Termoli, the nearest port on the mainland and twenty miles away, for it was obvious from the chart that we could not stay in the islands in anything but calm weather. There was no harbour, only a landing place – and no bad-weather anchorage.

With two overnight stops at anchor, we ran right down the coast and, an hour before sunrise, John sighted the islands silhouetted against the lightening eastern sky. As we passed through the channel, only eight hundred feet wide, between San Nicola and the tiny uninhabited island of Il Cretaccio, the run rose above the horizon. Three minutes later, as we came in sight of the landing, it was already blazing on the walled citadel perched so precariously – or so it seemed – on top of the two-hundred-and-fifty-feet-high San Nicola, which, at this point, is less than five hundred feet wide.

There, underneath the gate which gives access to the stone stairway leading up to the citadel, is a little pier where we manoeuvred the boat in between two others and tied her up.

San Nicola captured my heart instantaneously and completely. To some people, the houses, the one 'street' – which is nothing more than a wide, hundred-yard-long, stretch of ancient stone slabs worn smooth by countless thousands of feet over hundreds of years . . . the zig-zag road cut in the solid rock, the sun-drenched walls of the citadel, the age-old church with its belfry, perched at the top of the stairway – all these might seem rather decrepit and uncared-for. To me it was at once a place where one could find peace. A little walled town atop a tiny island. An island only just over three-quarters of a mile long and less than a quarter of a mile across at its widest part. An island to which, thank the gods, no one can bring a car and where nothing on wheels except, perhaps, a very small hard-cart can ascend the stone stairway to the stars. An island from where those teeming millions of troubled people who are so busy with living seemed utterly remote. Here, I knew, I would have time to live.

I had already persuaded John to stay in the islands for a couple of days, and while he went off in the dinghy to explore I stayed on San Nicola. In the afternoon I wandered down again to the little stone pier to watch the twice-weekly ferry from Manfredonia disembark its few passengers. It anchored about fifty yards off and the passengers came ashore in a couple of local boats.

One of the passengers – a girl of perhaps twenty-five or so, who had already turned off the jetty and was walking towards the gateway when I first noticed her – seemed vaguely familiar. I felt sure I had seen her before – or someone very much like her.

I watched her intently as she walked slowly along the foreshore path to the gate. Most of the other people were, by then, ahead of her, but she seemed to be lingering a little as if unsure of herself. Then, as she turned to go through the gateway, I caught a glimpse of her face. Yes, I had seen her before. Venice? Naples? No, I had met no one there whom I knew – and, besides, it was much longer ago than that, I was certain. England? Yes, London . . . all those years ago . . . this girl was so like Nicola, only a bit older of course.

I was intrigued and felt I must see her close to, and so I hurried along to the gateway and through to the stone stairs, but there were only the other people in sight a little way up. There *was* one woman here with similar build and clothes, but certainly not young. Perhaps I had been subconsciously thinking of Nicola and imagined all the rest. Strange, though

. . . and I felt a little uneasy for several hours afterwards, and I said nothing to John when I met him that evening to return to the yacht.

When, on the third day after our arrival, a rising wind made it imperative that the yacht should leave, I carried my bag ashore and said goodbye to John. I felt I could not leave this fascinating and carefree place just like that – nor so soon. Perhaps I had, all those years ago, fallen a little in love with Nicola, but there was no doubt at all that I had fallen very much in love with her island. John had to get back. Nearly six hundred miles of sea lay between him and Naples. The summer was passing and he had to get across to Termoli while the sea was reasonably calm.

So I wished him 'bon voyage' – and waved him goodbye as he rounded San Domino and passed out of my sight. I turned, and walked slowly through the gateway and up the stone stairs. John was going home. I was already there.

Not wishing to go over to San Domino to live in the hotel, I asked in the Post Office if they knew anyone who would put me up for a few months. They did. I moved in right away and was soon living happily with a local fisherman, Giorgio Galeazzi, and his wife Margherita, who most kindly provided me with any meals or packed lunches I wanted.

Summer, that year, lingered on. Days drifted by and I did little except wander or laze in the warm sunshine. Morning and evening, moonrise and moonset, followed each other in their timeless march – yet I had no conscious feeling of time passing, nor guilt at time wasted. Nothing, it seemed, could mar the real contentment and peace which I had found at last – or so it seemed.

It must have been about a month after John left that I happened to be down at the landing when the ferry came in. Most of the dozen or so arrivals were obviously holidaymakers who would shortly be taken across to the islands' only hotel on San Domino, but one of the passengers – a woman of perhaps between thirty and thirty-five years of age – was, I felt sure, a local resident. She did not look around when she stepped ashore, as a visitor would, but walked straight up the little pier and along the foreshore to the gate at the foot of the stone stairway, without turning her head.

As she herself turned to go through the gateway, she stumbled and the bundle she was carrying fell from her hand and rolled down the beach to within a few yards from where I was standing. I picked it up and walked up to the gateway and, as she went to take it from me, I saw her features clearly for the first time. Again I was swept back to the little Soho restaurant, and then suddenly to my first day on the island when I thought I had seen someone like Nicola – for this woman also reminded me of her.

Carrying her bundle, I walked beside her up the stone stairway to the citadel. She had just returned from her annual summer-holiday job as governess with an English family in Manfredonia and conversed easily in English. By the time we reached the top, three-quarters of an hour later, I had told her briefly how I had come to be in the Tremiti Islands but without mentioning Nicola by name. I asked her about herself. Her name, she told me, was Maria. Her mother had died when she was born, and she herself had been brought up by the local doctor and his wife whom, I gathered, she had long since come to regard as her real father and mother. She made no mention of any other father and I did not press the question.

About a week later, after I had spent the morning down on the beach near the landing place, I stopped for a rest a little way up the stairway and sat down, leaning against a rock. The sun was warm on my face, and I must have dozed a little, for I realized with a start that quite a number of people were passing me, going up to the citadel. The ferry had just come in.

I watched them idly – and then leapt to my feet. A girl had turned and looked at me as she passed . . . and she was the same girl I had seen on that first day. Her very walk – the way she moved her arms – the colour of her hair . . . everything about her was – Nicola. Yet I knew it must be just my imagination. The likeness was truly amazing – but I knew this was pure fantasy. Nicola would have been a woman of over thirty now. She had told me, I remembered, that her mother had died before she, Nicola, had gone to England and so it was unlikely, almost impossible, that there had been a much younger sister, although the only real difference between this girl and Nicola as I had known her – apart from the five years' or so discrepancy in their ages – was the look in her eyes. Nicola's had always had a fascinating twinkle and were full of happy laughter. The eyes of the girl beside me were full of fear, as if she was remembering something very frightening and was aware that she was about to experience it again.

Then she went ghostly white and staggered as if she was going to fall. But just then a man going down the stairway, and leading a donkey carrying two enormous panniers, forced us to make way for him, and we parted – she going to the right where there was a steep drop outside a low stone wall, and I to the left. Following the donkey were half a dozen laughing children, and when they had passed I found to my astonishment that I was alone. The girl was nowhere to be seen.

I turned, and looked down the steps, thinking she must have gone back, but I could see only the man and his donkey – and the children.

Puzzled, I looked over the wall and down the slope strewn with boulders. From where I stood, I had a clear view right down to the gateway, but the only living things there were a few goats grazing amongst the boulders. Thinking that she might possibly have been caught by one of the donkey's panniers and lost her balance, I scrambled over the wall and down the slope – but I was alone with the goats.

I was completely and utterly baffled at her disappearance.

Of course, I suppose I must have been thinking a lot more of Nicola, since I found her island, than I had realized – and maybe I had only imagined the girl. There had been a few women in front of her as she climbed up the stone stairs, but now they were out of sight round another bend, although I could just see their heads.

I gave it up. I could think of no rational explanation other than that she could, just conceivably, have hurried on while the children were passing and got in front of the other women.

I spent the whole of the next day wandering around in the citadel, but I saw nothing of the girl I had met – or thought I had met – and I did my best to dismiss the incident as a figment of my imagination. San Nicola was obviously casting its spell over me.

A few weeks later – by which time I had seen quite a lot of Maria, and both the doctor, Adrian Howard, and his French-born wife, Maryse, had become my very good friends – I was on my way down to the landing place, intending to spend the day in a small sailing-dinghy which I had borrowed from Giorgio. Rounding the bend in the stairway where I had sat and rested on that previous occasion, I came face to face with – Nicola. There was no doubt about it. This girl, suddenly halted in front of me, was Nicola – a few, perhaps five or six years older than when I knew her in London twenty years ago, but Nicola herself.

For a few moments I could do nothing but look. Then I clutched one of her hands in both mine – and almost let it go again in horror. It was icy, clammy cold. I looked earnestly at her face. She was smiling in recognition but her cheeks, her mouth, and even her eyes, were almost as if made from wax.

'Nicola,' I said, and bent forward to embrace her – but stopped, knowing (though how or why I know not) that her face, too, would be icy cold.

She stood smiling – but did not speak. Then, taking my hand in hers, she moved as if to continue her way up. We were only a few yards below the sharp bend in the zig-zag stairway. On her side the wall was low, and the sheer drop of perhaps thirty feet or so made it seem as if she was walking along the edge of a precipice. Suddenly, her hand seemed to melt away inside mine – and she was gone.

I stood there, rooted to the ground and trembling, and felt the cold perspiration forming on my forehead and on the back of my neck. It was as if I had just walked with and even touched a ghost, for my own hand – which a few moments before had held Nicola's – was now as icy cold as hers had been. She – if she it had been – had completely disappeared, and I wondered if I was losing my senses. Even the magic of the island – Nicola's island – no longer held me in its spell as I ran on up the stairway, stumbling as I went.

Passing under the castle entrance to the citadel, I paused exhausted, and stood there, panting, for what seemed hours.

By the time I reached Giorgio's cottage it was almost dark – and I was still very shaky, so I went on to the doctor's house silently praying that I would find someone there to whom I could talk. I felt I must tell someone of my strange and frightening experience.

To my intense relief, both the doctor and his wife, and Maria also, were there.

It was Maria who opened the door to me, and her scream – for I suppose I must have looked rather like a ghost myself – brought Adrian and Maryse running out from their living-room.

'Good God! what in Heaven's name is wrong?' Adrian said, as he led me to a chair. 'You look as if you could do with a stiff brandy.' After I had swallowed a good double in one gulp, I sat there, the fiery liquid burning my throat, and several more minutes passed before I was able to pour out my story.

I told them first how I had come to know Nicola. Then, as the rest of my strange tale unfolded, I noticed that all three of my listeners were making furtive glances at each other. Looking back, now, I believe I was aware already, then, that they all knew precisely what I was talking about and that my strange story was not really so strange to them.

For a minute or so, when I had finished, they looked at each other – each about to speak, and then hesitating ... each appearing to hope that one of the other two would speak first. Maria broke the silence. 'Yes,' she said, 'we know – I have seen her too,' and then she burst into tears. 'You tell him,' she sobbed, turning to Adrian.

'Nicola,' he said, 'is Maria's half-sister – although they met for the first time only about ten years ago. Maria is our adopted daughter, and she's lived with us ever since she was a baby. As you know, I believe, her mother – who was Nicola's mother, too – died when Maria was born. Maria never knew her own father, and Nicola – then five years old – was sent away to stay with her grandmother when Maria's birth was imminent and did not come back until after we adopted Maria. Nicola, in fact, did not know Maria even existed until her – Nicola's – own father told her shortly before he died in London.

'Nicola had no other relatives in England. She became very lonely after she had lost her father and decided to come back here to see her only "sister".

'That would have been about 1961, when Nicola was twenty-two and Maria seventeen, and they became extremely fond of each other as soon as they met. Both had inherited the beauty and charm of their mother, and while Nicola had some of her father's characteristics too, Maria was all of her mother – and no two sisters could have loved each other more.

'Nicola came to live with us when she came back to the island, and became as much our own daughter as Maria has. She often spoke about you and wished she had kept in touch – she was very fond of you, you know.'

'But where is she now?' I broke in, feeling extremely puzzled, 'and what did you mean, Maria,' I said, turning towards her, 'when you said, "Yes, we know – I have seen her too"?'

By this time Maria had recovered sufficiently to talk – otherwise I would not have broken in on Adrian's story. But the doctor was only too willing to let Maria tell me first-hand.

'When she first came back to San Nicola,' Marie said, 'we soon became quite inseparable, and for a whole year I was happier than I had ever been before.' Here she glanced at Adrian and Maryse, who were watching her intently, and managed a warm smile – which came more from her eyes than from her mouth, and which said more fervently than any words could have done, 'Oh! I've been so happy with you too, you know that – but I had found my very own sister at last, and that was a great joy to me.

'Then she had the accident. Coming up to the citadel one day the following summer – we were both larking about a bit – some children rushed down and went between us. Nicola stumbled towards the wall, lost her balance and fell over. We were just at that sharp bend where there is a steep drop and all those rocks. She must have fallen about thirty feet and struck her head.

'Some men coming down behind the children went down and brought her up, and then carried her back here.' She paused, near to tears again, and Adrian continued. 'She was unconscious,' he said, 'but outwardly unhurt except for the cut on her head. Whatever other injuries had been caused by her head striking the rock obviously required specialist treatment. I got her across to the hospital in Manfredonia on the next ferry . . . and there she still is. All efforts to bring her back to full consciousness have so far failed, but they feel sure there's no physical damage – nothing, at any rate, which can be restored by operation. It's more a mental condition.'

'But,' I interrupted, 'Maria says she's seen her . . . here on the island. How can . . .' Then Maria spoke again. 'Yes, she comes here often – looking exactly as she did that day, more than ten years ago. Usually I know – the night before the ferry comes in I dream that she's coming, and I go down to meet her. But I didn't know she was coming today. Last night, I did not go to sleep – I was sitting up with the old lady who lives near the church. We are taking it in turns – she's very ill.'

Maria paused for a moment. 'The last time I met her here,' she went on, 'was before I went to Manfredonia this summer. While I was there, I saw her every day in hospital, of course – just lying there – still unconscious. When I met her here last, we climbed the stairway together . . . always we get to that sharp bend where she fell – and then she just goes . . . disappears. It's awful. I'm sure I hear her cry of fear sometimes, as I did on that day so long ago. I take her hand, just as you did – and last time I thought she really would get past the bend. I know from my dreams that that is what she's trying to do – get past the place where she fell. Then she'd be all right again, I know. Perhaps we two – the two people she loves the most – together – perhaps with each of her hands held by someone she loves, and who loves her – perhaps, then, she'd be all right.'

'Can I go over and see her in the hospital?' I said. 'No' – and Maria's reply was hardly audible, even in that silent room, but there was no doubt of her firmness of mind. 'No,' she said, 'we'll meet her together next time – and then, perhaps, who knows, you can be really reunited.'

Two weeks went by before Nicola came to Maria again in her dream. 'There was no doubt,' she told me next day, 'Nicola remembered you and wanted us both to meet her. No, she doesn't actually speak to me, even in the dream. I just see her – and know what she wants to tell me.'

It seemed like eternity – waiting for the ferry to come in the following afternoon. I went down with Maria and waited inside the gateway. Coincidence had turned full circle, and I was about to meet Nicola again by appointment – but I had never before had an appointment with a ghost, and hardly dared hope that, as Maria had predicted, she would actually come and walk with me up the stone stairway.

Several people had come off the ferry and through the gateway before we saw her. Not that she was really among the half-dozen or so men and women passing through the arched gateway, but both of us became aware, at the same instant, that she was there. Smiling wanly, she took one of our hands in each of hers – again I was struck by the icy cold of her flesh – and we turned about, walking slowly up towards the citadel.

She looked exactly the same as when I had first encountered her but her smile, as she turned first towards Maria and then towards me, was warmer. No, not warmer – not from that cold, waxen but oh so beautiful face – but loving, for here she was close to the two people she loved the most in the world.

As we neared the sharp bend where she had fallen, her icy grip tightened on our hands and the smile on her face turned into a look of grim determination. All the world seemed to stand still for a moment, and the only sounds of which we were conscious were those of our feet on the rock beneath us.

Then we were past the fateful spot. The world seemed to come alive again and we both looked at Nicola. Her eyes were closed – but her face was in complete repose, like that of a child whose mother has just tucked her up for the night after reading her favourite bedtime story.

Gradually the grip on my hand slackened and I could tell by the look on Maria's face, as I glanced across at her in front of Nicola, that she had felt the same change. Then, as if by some silent command, we took Nicola's hands in ours again, but already they felt softer and warmer, and within seconds they seemed to melt away . . . and Nicola herself was gone.

Maria and I stood speechless. Then a great feeling of relief came over me – and over her, too, I know – and we smiled triumphantly at each other. Our mission had been completed. Nicola was going to recover.

As we passed beneath the old archway and re-entered the citadel, the ancient church clock chimed the hour. It was four o'clock.

A few hours later, as we were sitting together with Adrian

and Maryse, talking about Nicola . . . and wondering . . . and hoping, the telephone rang. Maria was wanted by the hospital in Manfredonia

We could tell by the look on her face, when she came back into the room, what the news had been. Nicola had miraculously regained consciousness. She had not spoken yet but was out of the coma. She had opened her eyes shortly before four o'clock that afternoon.

Another telephone-call the following morning told us that the crisis was over. Her mind was, naturally, very hazy but she had asked for both Maria and me.

We had to wait two days for the next ferry. They were forty-eight hours of mounting excitement . . . and when, at last, we were both at the door of the ward, and the Sister said we could go in, I could hardly contain myself.

It is now two months later, as I finish writing this in my room at Giorgio's. Tomorrow I am bringing Nicola home.

We are to be married in three weeks' time in the old church under the belfry – at four o'clock in the afternoon.

THE LOCKET

by Laurence Grafftey-Smith

WHEN old Madame de Pavillac died, her three daughters found themselves with some farmland, a hundred hectares of forest, and a château that had been the family home for nearly five hundred years. There was no way of dividing the estate without selling the house, and nobody wanted to pay the price the sisters asked. Their agent suggested letting the château 'to some rich Americans'; and it was to Pavillac, now rented by my friends the Ogilvies, that I was invited for a summer holiday, after a more than usually exhausting season on Broadway.

I was looking forward to the visit. Donald Ogilvie and I were friends at Yale, and Anne was acting with me in a revival of *Saint Joan* when they first met. I cannot share Donald's enthusiasm for manoeuvring masses of marble into surrealist shapes; but he can afford his hobby, and it hurts no one. I particularly wanted to see Penelope, my god-daughter, again, for I thought of her not only as an adorable child but also as a great artist in the making. Charles Lemesle, who had had her at the piano since she was five, had told me that there was very little more he could teach her.

I drove down from the coast, stopping the night at Vendôme, and reached Pavillac next afternoon. Like so many villages in the Dordogne, it nestles on the slope of a hill; and the few primitive shops clustered round the smithy suggested no adequate congregation for the great church, whose Romanesque door and windows dominate the tiny Place Gambetta. I was instructed to keep straight on and take an avenue on the left, round the curve of the hill. This avenue mounted, twisting and turning through the woods for about a mile, before bringing me to the château; and I had to cross a genuine water-lilied moat by a no less authentic drawbridge to reach the gravel sweep in front of the house. I had a confused impression of towers, and of a long mullioned façade in the golden stone of the region, before Donald and Anne came running to bid me welcome.

They were both in great form. Anne was looking better than I had seen her for years, and Donald was full of plans for putting a north light into an enormous barn and using it as a studio. When Anne had told me all about the walled kitchen-garden, and the unexpectedly efficient plumbing, and the family retainers, I asked where my god-daughter was.

'I hope the château runs to a harpsichord or something for her,' I said.

'Oh! I thought Donald had told you about Penny,' said Anne, suddenly serious.

'I thought Anne had written to you,' said Donald.

'Why? Is anything wrong?'

'Nothing's really wrong.' Donald was very emphatic. 'But she was taking too much out of herself and has to have a rest.'

'It was Lemesle who noticed it first,' Anne explained. 'He told us that Penny's music was burning her up. That's how he put it. She always was completely – what's the word? – absorbed. You remember that week in Stockholm. But lately it got so that she couldn't bear to be doing anything else. And I found she wasn't sleeping properly. You haven't seen her for some time, David. Technically, and artistically, she's developed in the most remarkable way.'

'Composition, believe it or not,' said Donald, interrupting. 'Extraordinary stuff. Completely mature. Lemesle says . . .'

'Lemesle says it frightens him,' said Anne. 'It's miles away from her age and experience. She's only fourteen, after all. We felt we had to have an opinion, of course, and the specialist seemed to understand at once. He insisted on Penny having at least six months away from all music, just running wild. He said it might even have to be two years. There's not a piano in the house. Not even a wireless set, or a record-player.'

We were sitting in the great drawing-room, looking out over the poplar-green valley of the Dordogne. The light seemed suddenly to have dimmed in the sky.

'How's she taking all this?' I asked anxiously. The thought of Penny condemned to live in a world without music was a tragic one.

'She couldn't be sweeter or more reasonable,' Donald assured me. 'Lemesle handled her beautifully. He told her that a longish pause now would be the very best thing, not only for her but for her music. He advised her to go away and fill herself to the brim with sunshine and pinewoods and goat-cheese and fairy stories and Monbazillac – that's our local wine, rather good.' He saw my raised eyebrows and added, 'One glass with each meal!'

'Anyway,' said Anne, 'she's a different girl already.'

'You asked where she was,' continued Donald. 'Ten to one you'll find her down by the swimming-pool, in the woods. She bathes and sunbathes every day, and looks pretty good on it.'

'I'll go and find her,' I said, getting up. 'I have a little present for her.'

But at that moment, Penny came running into the room. As soon as she saw me, she jumped into my arms. I was kissed on the nose, the mouth and both ears.

'Lovely! Lovely!' she kept saying. 'Oh, Uncle David! It's really and truly lovely to see you again. How long can you stay?'

I told her that I had no job until they began filming *Nightshade* in October, and that I was there until her Papa threw me out. Then I took a small tissue-paper parcel from my pocket.

'Here!' I said. 'Something to remind you that you're almost an old lady now.'

It was only a little necklace of seed-pearls, but I had fallen for it at sight. Penny loved it. It was early eighteenth-century French work, and it carried a gold and enamel locket, containing a curl of faded yellow hair. Penny went straight to the mirror and put it on, admiring herself unashamedly.

I watched her. I was not happy at what I saw.

She was, indeed, a different girl from the Penelope I had seen two years before. She had grown, of course, and gracefully. Her bright corn hair, worn in two long plaits, were already darker than the spun gold I remembered, in spite of the bleach of the sun. It was her eyes that worried me: slate-blue and dark-lashed, they looked too big for her face. I didn't know whether this was a symptom of too much music or too little; but they were the eyes of a woman, of an unhappy woman; they were not the eyes of a fourteen-year-old girl.

'Has this locket got a story?' she asked, 'or must we make one up ourselves?'

'I only know that that's the de Pavillac crest on the back of it,' I answered. 'I found that out in the shop in London. It was too much of a coincidence altogether: I just had to get it for you. You can make up any story you like about the lady who first wore it, but you can be pretty sure she wore it here, in Pavillac.'

She studied the little thing carefully.

'Here's a sort of dragon with a crown,' she said. 'We've got him all over the place in the house here. And what does this stand for?'

'The lady's initial, I suppose. V for Valentine; V for Véronique; V for whatever it was.'

'You realize, I hope,' she said solemnly, 'that it's the nicest present I've ever had? Now I must go and show it to everybody.' She ran from the room.

Except at dinner-time, I didn't see much of Penny for the next few days. She spent her time somewhere down in the woods, while Anne or Donald in turn, or both of them, launched me on local society or took me to see the sights of the neighbourhood. Every day brought new delight. Donald had a passion for the Périgord castles; Biron, Beynac, and Bonaguil; he peopled them with troubadours and joustings. Anne and I preferred the rivers, those dreaming Dordogne rivers, moving somnambulant through the poplar-trees. But I had to plead for a rest from tourist activity and from the gargantuan luncheons of the local squirearchy.

So it must have been a week or ten days before I explored Penny's neck of the woods. It was late afternoon. Anne showed me the general line of my way from the dining-room window, and as I followed path after path rustling with dry leaves, down cathedral-aisles of beech and oak, I found myself resenting the outrage of a modern swimming-pool in this green peace. I need not have worried. I turned my last corner and came to a clearing in the forest, where huge trees stood in a circle round a rush-fringed lake. The air became suddenly very still, and I had a strange feeling that I was intruding, as if I were interrupting something. I could see no path continuing into the woods beyond the lake. The world came to an end there.

Penny, naked as a goldfish, was lying on the grass, her arms outflung behind her head, smiling at the sun. She had not heard me coming. I didn't want to embarrass her, so I stepped quietly back into the wood and came out again, whistling. She made a swoop for a towel and fixed it before she looked up to see who it was.

'Well, Uncle David!' she cried, 'at last you've come! And high time, too!' She patted the turf hospitably. I sat down by her side.

'This towel was in case you were the gardener,' she saw fit to explain.

'Good idea, keep it on!' I said hastily. 'Oughtn't you to be wearing sun-glasses?'

'The sun never bothers me!' she replied.

If one could forget those eyes, she certainly was the picture of health. She was toasted all over to a warm apricot russet. Her strong young hands and that little ripple of muscle between her shoulders were part of her pianist's equipment. But her eyes were now shadowed with dark lines, lines which had not been there when I came to Pavillac. The contrast of the young face and those fever-rimmed eyes was the more shocking because Penny seemed to be entirely happy and carefree, laughing and chattering like any school-girl of her age.

'Daddy's just crazy about his old barn, isn't he?' she was saying. 'It's because it has big double-doors going right up to the roof. Did he tell you he's planning to sculpt something really monumental, a group of Druids? We have a dolmen here, you know. But no one knows what Daddy's Druids will look like when he's finished with them!'

'Penelope Ogilvie!' I said, 'that's an unfilial remark.'

She was silent for a moment, and I felt again how abnormally still everything seemed. There was no singing of birds; there was no whisper of leaves in the trees. The sun beat down, unveiled by any cloud, and the sky lay molten blue in the mirror of the lake. Even the reeds were motionless. Heat and light were both so pure and so intense they ceased to be familiar experiences; they became symbols of some elemental phenomenon. And a nagging impression of expectancy in the silence was insistent.

'I hate to go,' said Penny, 'but I think perhaps we ought to get back to the house. Isn't it about your time for tea or a drink or something? The sun will soon be gone behind those trees.'

She slipped on a bright scarlet bathrobe and began collecting her odds and ends, wrapping knitting-needles and some light-blue wool carefully in a silk scarf.

'Something very, very secret, for Mummy's birthay,' she explained, smiling. 'She mustn't see it yet.' Then the smile died from her face, which blurred and suddenly became a mask.

'There's quite a lot that that unpleasant bitch must not

see, besides my knitting!' she said. 'Because now I know a lot of things – such a lot of things . . .' Her voice had become deeper, oilier. She laughed, but it was a stupid, evil giggle of complicity.

'Penny!' I cried, 'Penny!'

She looked up at me, blinking. The mask wavered and broke, like sunlight in water. Youth and innocence flowed back into her face.

'You're looking very serious all of a sudden!' she said. 'I'll race you through the wood. Bet you I get to the house first!' She was off into the trees like a startled dryad.

I could not follow her until I had sat down for a moment on the flower-spangled turf. The trees and the lake and all the air around me throbbed in the burning silence. Once more I had the feeling that here the world came to an end.

I said nothing to the Ogilvies. I did not know what to say. I wanted time to think things over.

Penny was completely and charmingly herself all the evening. She duly trumped her partner's ace – an old habit of hers – when we played Family Bridge before her very early bedtime. I began to wonder whether I had had some sort of hallucination, and I slept badly. It was while I was looking out at the moonlit garden behind the château around four in the morning, wishing I had brought some sleeping-pills, that I saw a little figure slipping from shadow to shadow between the trees and over the lawn, back to the shelter of the house. I could not swear it was Penny, but I knew it could be no one else.

I was having my coffee and *brioches* in bed when she came into my room next morning. She was wearing the scarlet bathrobe, but she shook it off as she reached out and stole one of my *brioches*. I was relieved to observe a notional but adequate bikini.

'What do you think this is, Uncle David? she asked, nibbling daintily. She leaned forward to show me her left shoulder. I saw a thick slug-shaped red mark, an inch long, and it was on, rather than in, the sunburnt skin; it looked like some sort of incrustation.

'I woke up with it,' she explained. 'Daddy thinks I must have got stung yesterday, but they don't have poison-ivy in France, do they? And it looks much too big for an insect-bite. I know it wasn't there when I had my bath last night.'

I remembered a stealthy return to the house, shortly before dawn.

'Does it hurt much?' I asked.

'It sort of tingles,' she said. 'You couldn't call it really painful. And, anyway, I think it's getting better fast.'

'I'll kiss it and make it all well,' I said lightly, bending my face to her shoulder. Then I started back as if I had been stung myself. They say that memories of smells are of all the most evocative. I was instantly back at the cattle-branding on my grandfather's ranch in Texas. The mark on Penny's shoulder was the scar of a deep and very recent burn. And it was fading before my eyes.

'I wouldn't worry about it, if I were you,' I said with some difficulty. 'It seems to be going away. Are you off to the pool already? Is there any sun there now?'

'It's a real sun-trap. All day long. Perhaps that's why the Druids had their dolmen there.'

'Oh!' I said. 'Is that where it is!'

'In the trees, on the other side of the pool. It's not much to look at, really. Just some old stones and a little underground room. Are you coming down with me?' She put on her robe again.

For reasons of my own I wanted to go, very much, and I was going to tell her so; but I decided to stay away. I said I had letters to write and would come and fetch her for lunch. I was thinking hard. As she turned to the door, I made up my mind.

'Tell me, Penny darling,' I said, and my own voice sounded strange to me, 'what do you like best about Pavillac? What do you like best of all? Your mother says' – I repeated the words slowly – 'your mother says ... your mother says ...' I waited.

It worked. It happened. It was horrible.

Her face blurred, like wax melting, and seemed to reshape

itself into an expression of vicious cunning. Her pigtails were swinging over her scarlet bathrobe. She caught them and tugged them, and then she began unplaiting them.

'What I most love is learning about things,' she said, in that new, oily voice. 'It's wonderful. Quite different from my music. I think you know what I mean, Uncle David; I can guess that. But you can only know a little; my friend knows everything. I've only known him for one little week and it seems like a hundred days.' She paused. 'Like a hundred and twelve days,' she said, looking at me as if she were saying something important; 'a hundred and twelve days. But if you say a word about it to that human sow you mentioned just now, I'll ask my friend to hurt you. Or to tell me how I can hurt you.'

I heard myself shouting, 'Penny, come back! Penny! For Christ's sake, come back!'

Her face changed as I watched her, and she was suddenly Penny again, laughing in surprise to find her pigtails were half-loosened.

'Till lunch-time, then!' she cried. 'And don't dare be late!' She blew me a kiss and was gone.

I dressed quickly and found my way to the big barn, where Donald was busy discussing with the blacksmith details of the new glazing in the roof. I asked him to get Anne to come downstairs at once. A few minutes later we were all sitting on the terrace, round a flimsy wicker table under a gaudy beach-umbrella, and I was trying to tell them about Penny. It wasn't easy. They looked at each other puzzled, and then they looked at me as if I were out of my mind. They didn't seem to understand a word I said. I may well have been a little incoherent; I was very frightened.

At last Donald realized that I was desperately serious. He ground his cigarette out distastefully.

'Are you telling us,' he said, 'that Penny spends her time at the pool flirting with some village Don Juan? If so, I don't believe a word of it; but we can easily find out. I can see you're worried, David. I'm quite sure you're absolutely wrong!'

'That isn't what I've been trying to tell you at all,' I said impatiently.

'But I thought you said . . .' Anne began.

'Tell me all about Pavillac,' I said, interrupting her. 'Is that dolmen authentic?'

'It's listed as a *monument historique*; that's all I know.'

'Is it, perhaps, on the site of some earlier temple?' I asked.

'That seems most unlikely,' he replied. 'There was a temple of Venus somewhere near here, I believe; there are Gallo-Roman remains all over the Dordogne. But all that would be rather later than the Druids, not earlier. Their dolmen may, of course, have been used for worship, in Roman times. What's the idea?'

'Just that I don't think Penny's new friend is a local character,' I said. 'Or a summer visitor, for that matter. And I'm sure that what's going on is something much worse than a girlish flirtation. That's why I must know about Pavillac, whether it has any special history, legends, anything. I want to know what influences – if that's the right word – what influences may exist near that pool or in that corner of the woods.'

'Oh, my God!' cried Anne, and began biting her knuckles. 'L'Estropié!'

I looked at her, puzzled.

'What Anne has just remembered,' Donald explained, 'is that a most unpleasant man called Gilles de Pavillac lived here in the early 1700s: a Huysmanic character. He murdered his wife, very horribly. And he had men stealing children for him to torture and use, boys and girls, from all the villages around. No one dared complain, of course, in those days. He was a cripple from birth: that's why he was called L'Estropié. Our village curé, who is the local antiquarian, says that he still . . .' He stopped unexpectedly and shook his head angrily.

'You know, I just can't take all this very seriously,' he declared. 'Not in relation to Penny. I know Penny. And Anne knows Penny. Much better, David, than you possibly can. And it doesn't make sense!'

But I saw that Anne was shaken. She stared at me in distress.

'According to you, the child hates me!' she cried.

'You know I wouldn't hurt either of you for the world. Try to be patient with me for a moment,' I pleaded. 'Try to accept as possible, as just possible, that there may be something evil down by that pool. It has a very special atmosphere, as you may know, and a lot seems to have happened there: blood-sacrifices, and God knows what pagan erotica. Try to accept as possible what I think is certain, that Penny, with her acutely developed sensitivities; Penny, now that her natural climate of music is denied her, must be abnormally susceptible to whatever influence this something, or somebody, radiates. At this moment, Penny is hopelessly vulnerable. One might say that, without music, she is, spiritually, a vacuum. She must be as sensitive to any and every strong psychological impression as a film is to sunlight.'

Anne started to say something, but I did not stop.

'I don't think you and I would see anything,' I continued, 'if we went to the pool; but who knows what, or who, appears to Penny? And I'm afraid we must certainly say "who". There may not be any words actually spoken but who knows what Penny hears? You tell me of an eighteenth-century sadist, L'Estropié; if there is some evil atmosphere there, he may, of course, be the cause. I am suggesting that, down there, everything conspires to evil. It might not matter to anyone else, but it is poison for Penny. Poison!'

I suddenly remembered the little locket with the de Pavillac crest.

'Donald!' I cried, 'ring up the curé, quick! Ask him what was the name of the wife of Gilles de Pavillac; the woman he murdered.'

He ran to the hall, and we heard him shouting for the

number. I saw Anne looking at me, and I remembered her tragic cry.

'Darling Anne,' I said, 'try not to worry about yourself. Penny's growing up, and she may be jealous of you, without knowing it. If I'm right about that pool, whatever experience she is having must bring many strange things to the surface. Her mood of jealousy will pass, but it is strong now. So strong that it serves as a key to that other mood. It will pass, if we are in time.'

'If we're in time?' Donald in the doorway echoed my words. 'Why? Do you think . . .?'

'What was that woman's name, Donald?' I said.

'According to the curé, Virginie.'

'Oh, my God!' I said. For I knew now what I had done. Perhaps she had been wearing the locket when he killed her. V for Virginie . . .

Druids and temples of Venus seemed simple and innocent now, compared with the malign spirit I had attracted back to the pool. Through that little locket, as directly as if it were a burning-glass, I had focused hell-fire upon my darling girl.

The Ogilvies were staring at me.

'Can't you see?' I cried. 'Can't you see we must get Penny back to the house and out of Pavillac at once?'

'You run on!' said Donald. 'Hurry! I'm going up to get my gun. You never know!'

I tore off down the path through the wood, with Anne behind me. I heard her fall, and saw her pick herself up painfully; but I dared not stop to help her.

Penny, apricot-russet on the green grass, was lying on her side, her back to the pool. One of her pigtails was caught up on a large thistle. She was dead. There were thick slug-shaped red marks all over her face and throat and neck, and her mouth was shapeless with burns. There were the same scars of horrid kisses from the pit where the locket should have hung, and there was another area of major burns. The necklace had been torn off her; the seed-pearls were scattered on the grass. The locket, now open and empty, was some way away. It had been deeply pressed – stamped, apparently – into the earth, and at that one point the grass was scorched and blackened.

I heard Anne coming. I just had time to throw the scarlet bathrobe over the body, and to close those tragic eyes, before she limped out of the wood, sobbing with pain and crying, 'Penny! Penny!'

A SELF-POSSESSED WOMAN

by Julian Barnes

I HAVE always disliked those large blocks of flats at the northern end of Baker Street. They epitomize for me the deadness of high material comfort. Sherwin Mansions is no exception. You hit carpet as soon as you leave the street; double swing doors isolate you still further, like the transparent plastic flaps in hospital corridors; and round every corner you glimpse a distant, unconvincing fountain coddled by greenery on which the rain will never fall. I became even more bad-tempered.

'Waste of time.'

'More of a waste to go back now you've come this far.'

Contestable; but I only protested by silence. Robert was, after all, a friend, more or less; and was also, less questionably, a business associate. He'd been providing me for years with young authors who, he would assure me, were just the thing to brighten up the spring list of a staid university press. Such attempts to diversify were, it is true, rarely disastrous: the bright young things sold no worse than their duller, older colleagues; but until one of them turned out to be the sleeper of the year, I would have little cause to disguise my feelings from Robert.

'I mean, L.U.P., after all? Why not . . . Dennis Wheatley's lot?'

'Firstly,' said Robert, well-prepared, 'Because this is real. And secondly' (with ironic deference), 'because this is just what you need . . .'

'. . . to brighten my list.'

'Quite.'

An eye inspected us from the middle of the doors; latches clicked. 'Mr. Beesley,' said Robert, 'Philip Euchre, of L.U.P.' The carpet got thicker as we filed after him into a large sitting-room. Mrs. Beesley extended a hand from her arm-chair: 'I'm afraid I can't get up easily. I appear to have slipped a disc.' A glass of iced water was balanced on one arm of her chair.

For a medium, she disappointed me a little. Soberly dressed, lightly made up, enjoyable to look at; above all, she was young. I had expected something middle-aged and menopausal, compensating for the loss of her children by creating new life in the only way now open to her. Mrs. Beesley spurned my stereotype. She was perhaps twenty-five, very composed, interested but by no means over-impressed by meeting a publisher and a literary agent, and she participated in conversational preliminaries with Robert with an ironic detachment which probably exceeded his own.

I cast my eye round the collection of books, instinctively noting whether they were for use or display. Here, they were not dressed by the right according to size; individual volumes of sets were occasionally misplaced; a few bookmarks protruded. Use, then; or extremely cunning display.

'Well, Philip?' began Robert.

'Well, Mrs. Beesley?' I turned to her, encouraging but sceptical.

'I first became aware of my powers six months ago. Since then I have received the spirits of forty-two dead writers. They possess my mind and they communicate through my hand. They come to me on Friday evenings, between seven and eight. They never stay more than an hour. When they have gone, I feel myself again, quite soon.'

I waited; but it seemed that she had finished.

'How do you explain it?'

'I don't.'

'How long have you been ... interested in psychic ... phenomena?'

'They've never interested me at all – until now.'

'Why between seven and eight?'

'I don't know.'

'And when you write down what they say, what does the handwriting look like?'

'My own.'

'And you expect me to publish . . . communications?'

'As you please. This meeting is at Mr. Tyerman's request, not mine.'

I turned to her husband. 'And what do you do during these seances?'

'I don't think seance is quite the right word, Mr. Euchre. Sometimes I'm there, sometimes not. It doesn't make any difference, as long as I keep quiet.'

'What does Mrs. Beesley look like while she's possessed?'

'Much as she does now, except that she sits at her desk over there. But I don't get too close to her, in case I disturb the spirits.'

I was disappointed, even allowing for my low expectations. It sounded like a chummy reunion in a local. They weren't even trying to impress me with anything strange. Either they didn't mind whether I believed them or not, or they had made an accurate calculation of how to arouse my interest.

'Then perhaps I could see the . . . documents?'

There were about eighty sheets of paper, closely covered with slighty fey italics. Each page was dated, and had a red circle at the bottom for the spirit's name. I riffled through: Henry James, Coleridge, Gissing, Byron, John Cowper Powys, Landor, and so on. Some of the names I had never heard of. Some of the circles were empty, some of the attributions were followed by question marks.

'So they don't all tell you who they are?'

'No; sometimes we have to try and work it out from what they say.'

'They're all men, I see.'

'Yes.'

'What does it feel like' (I was fed up with her polite precision), 'to have Lord Byron inside you?'

Not a flicker. 'I'm not conscious of who the spirit is. I am conscious only of being possessed. I have no thoughts at the time, and no emotions more specific than an overall sense of exhilaration. I don't know what they say till I see what I've written.'

I felt reproved; also off balance. I found myself liking the Beesleys for the way in which they had ignored my abusive tone; and I was pleased that they were far from the vulgar charlatans I had expected. On the other hand, this made me even more convinced that they must be bogus. All in all, I was considerably intrigued. I asked to borrow the documents, and left with Robert.

'What did you think of her?' he asked.

'I thought she was a very . . . self-possessed woman.'

'Ha. And her discoveries?'

'I think the whole thing's as bogus as I did when we arrived. She just sits down and writes out parodies, that's what I think. There's no mumbo-jumbo, hands under the table in the dark stuff, because they're too intelligent for that. But it's still a put-up job. The other possibility is that she's a well-read hysteric who lies to imagine that men are taking over her body.'

'But what would it look like,' said Robert protractedly, 'if it were genuine?'

To that I had no immediate answer.

The next few days were full of young lecturers intent on choosing their own typefaces, middle-aged lecturers wondering why their advances weren't larger, and old professors inventing excuses for not delivering their manuscripts on time. It wasn't until the weekend that I pulled out the Beesley folder. It was to prove a great surprise.

I knew all the great stories of literary hoaxes – Chatterton, Macpherson, Ireland, Steevens – and was familiar with literary parodies, both when they are deliberate, and when (as is more usual in my business) they merely indicate the stylistic uncertainty of some debutant author. But the Beesley papers seemed to be of a different order. There were, as I expected, finished passages of prose and verse in the style of the authors to whom they were attributed. But there was much that was random: rough sketches, corrections to published work, explanations, arguments to be used in essays; there was even a series of limericks (obscene from 'Norman Douglas', obscurely libellous from 'James Joyce').

Halfway through the pile I came across a letter from Thackeray, complaining about Trollope's treatment of him in the *English Men of Letters* series. I dialled Robert and told him what I had found. 'So?' was his only reply. 'Come on, Robert, Thackeray snuffed it years before the series started.' 'So?' was still his comment, this time almost superior; then, 'Read on, Philip, and I'll be round in an hour.'

I read on, and saw a pattern. At first, the communications from the spirits (to go along with the hypothesis) were straightforward, and readily identifiable, as if it was a question of establishing good faith. Then, beginning with the Thackeray letter, some of the communications began to relate forward from the author's death: Henry James protesting that Ford Madox Ford's stories about him were 'not, in a manner of speaking, entirely redolent of veracity'; or Rupert Brooke complaining sarcastically that Churchill had written him a foolish panegyric for an obituary. The last paper was even more singular: dated the previous Friday, it was a harangue by D. H. Lawrence accusing Leavis of misrepresenting him.

Robert smiled at my expression as I opened the door to him.

'I'm only serious because I'm still looking for the flaw.'

'Maybe there isn't one?'

'Come on, you don't believe this any more than I do. It's just that, if we were dealing with a book, we could test the paper, look at the watermark or something. Here all the "evidence" is internal.'

'It's still evidence.'

'But there must be some test we can do.'

'Send off a few of the papers to relevant experts. Just send the early stuff, which isn't particularly controversial. Say they're transcripts of papers which someone has sent you, and could they be genuine. That way you won't commit yourself and you won't prejudice the response. Let the Beesleys know what you're doing, but don't tell them who's getting what.'

It was less than ideal; but it seemed the best thing to do in the circumstances.

The following Friday, Robert and I returned to Sherwin Mansions. Mrs. Beesley was still seated by her glass of water. The flat was just as claustrophobic as I had remembered it; outside, there was only an angled view of more blocks of flats; inside, the walls could barely be seen for books. Everything contrived to enclose one.

'I hear that you are slightly less sceptical, Mr. Euchre?' she began.

'Well, more puzzled anyway. If you're trying to deceive me, I can't see your motive: there won't be any money in it to speak of, even if we were to publish these things; though I suppose you might get some pleasure from fooling the literary world. If you're genuine, and the pieces are genuine, then all I can say is that a large number of people are going to be severely discountenanced, and if the Leavis piece is anything to go by, a lot of critics are going to have the extraordinary experience of being pursued by the dead.'

'That can't be all bad,' said Robert, excitedly, in an American accent.

'My husband is an adequately rich man,' said Mrs. Beesley, 'and my feelings towards writers, dead and alive, are almost wholly benevolent.' She said it plainly and seriously, as people do when they are lying well.

At seven o'clock it was time for Mrs. Beesley to start entertaining. She moved across to her desk with some difficulty, and sat down. I was on one side of her, Robert and Mr. Beesley on the other. She laid out several sheets of paper, and took up a pen. There was total stillness. After a few minutes she began to write, slowly and neatly. Apart from a slight tautening of the skin between her eyebrows, a slight drawing in of her cheeks towards the bone, she remained impassive. She might have been working out her bills, or composing a piece of advice to an unhappy child. In fact, as we discovered, it was an enthusiastic description by Aldous Huxley of the experience of dying under LSD.

'You knew it was Huxley?'

'No.'

'But you heard a voice of some sort?'

'No – I told you last time, I don't hear voices. I just feel . . . concentrated, in some way.'

'You knew you were writing, at least?'

'Oh, yes; but I follow the ink, I don't, and can't, follow the sense. It feels more as if I'm making a sort of pattern. I rise and fall with the letters.'

'And so you think that was Huxley?'

'Who do you think it was?'

I found myself yielding to the possibility of belief. I am as empirical as the next man. I rumbled Santa at eight and God at fifteen, and am heavily resistant to mind-readers, faith-healers, fortune-tellers, hypnotists, magicians and priests. Extraordinary coincidences prove to me only that there are extraordinary coincidences. The present set of circumstances, I admitted, I could not immediately explain. My liking for the Beesleys made me want to believe that they were genuine. Moreover, I was not being asked to accept more than a single set of facts: that the dead are not dead, that the dead can communicate with the living, that the dead know what is going on among the living. Put that way, it sounded a lot. But it was less than, say, being shown a miracle and then asked to accept a religion and a morality.

My own behaviour, and most of my beliefs, were threatened only tangentially.

'If this is true...' I began. Robert smiled; the Beesleys waited. '... and if we – you – can go on getting messages like this, then, to coin a phrase, the entire history, content, and criticism of literature will be overturned.'

'We could find out who Mr. W. H. was,' said Robert, 'or what was in Byron's memoirs, or what happened to Edwin Drood. Now do you see why I wanted a scholarly publisher to handle it?'

'Yes I do. But there's more to it, isn't there. It's not just that we can finish off unfinished works, and discover new ones. It changes the whole structure of things, doesn't it? If Thackeray, say, can now disapprove of Joyce, then that makes everything circular, not linear any more. Everyone is placed at the edge of a perfect circle – or maybe a sphere – looking inwards.'

'Provided,' said Robert, lightly sarcastic, 'that the papers are genuine.'

'Robert,' I replied seriously, 'what would it look like if they were?'

After that evening, Robert and I took to calling more frequently on the Beesleys – regularly on Fridays, and often on another day as well. They became, in due course, Ellen and William. They were always welcoming, though slightly reserved, and the fact that I was presumably at some point going to offer them a contract did not inhibit our friendship. Ellen, we discovered, had more trouble with her back than we had realized. She suffered a regular ache, with occasional spasms of extreme pain. Doctors refused to confirm her own diagnosis of a slipped disc, and made her go into hospital for a more extensive examination.

Meanwhile, the replies to my inquiries began to come in.

They were, at first, only partially encouraging; and I was frequenty irritated by the inability of academics to answer any straight question without first looking all round to see if the straightness wasn't an illusion. On further reflection, though, I had to admit that for once their suspicions were justified.

Three of the replies refused to make any comment. 'Scholarship,' ran one rebuke, 'does not consist in the intuitive assignment by a hyper-sensitive expert of some random passage of writing to a definite source. I would need to know the provenance of the manuscript, the circumstances of its discovery, the estimated date and likely author of the copy, before I could begin to assess who wrote the original, and when, and where.'

None of the replies, however, suggested forgery, or even parody, as the solution to the texts; and some were plainly encouraging. 'Might well be part of a Dickens letter – from his American trip, at a guess.' 'Certainly the sort of thing Johnson might have said when Boswell was not around: who was the traitor this time?' There were some positive identifications. 'Typical of the sort of inspired silliness one gets in the later (and earlier!) Carlyle.' Even – 'I suggest you send this off to *Notes and Queries* at once.'

But the clinching letter, as far as I was concerned, came from Professor Hirsh of Princeton, probably the leading expert on Arthur Hugh Clough. I had sent him the longest piece of manuscript produced by Ellen, and was rewarded with:

> Dear Mr. Euchre,
>
> Thank you for your letter of January 27th and its enclosure, which I found truly astounding. Normally, I would write and tell you how I really could not comment until I knew where the manuscript came from, and so on, and dig in behind a defensive palisade in the best traditions of scholarship. Instead, let me say that your manuscript represents the most exciting breakthrough I have had in the last ten years, and that I have not the slightest doubt as to its authenticity. It is clearly part of the missing volume of Clough's manuscript journals, which are

deposited in the University of California. The missing volume is known to cover those vital years of 1847–50 which are, at present, exiguously documented. Your discovery, I need hardly say, is of first-rate value. Where (I feel I may now ask) was it made? And how much more of the journal did you recover?

Supported by this letter, I felt able to take on my four fellow-directors at L.U.P. at our next weekly meeting. I presented the discovery to them in the form of a narrative, hoping that their initial reactions would be overcome, as mine had been, as the story unfolded. Hirsh's letter ensured me of a serious hearing, and I was relieved at the lightness of tone of the first few comments.

'So that's what they mean by ghosting, eh?' from Purdy; and, 'Hammer Films buying the rights, are they, Philip?' from MacMichael, the chairman. Then the heavier arguments came rolling in.

'Are you seriously suggesting, Philip, that after fifteen years building up a reputation in the academic world, L.U.P. should cast it to the four winds by publishing the . . . ravings of some madwoman?'

'Can you imagine the reviews? Good ones in *Psychic News* and *Rolling Stone*, and a panning all the way from the *Statesman* to the *T.L.S.*'

'Well, that's not very far.'

'It damn well is for us.'

'Where would it fit in our list, Philip?'

'Make a special category for it – it's a special book. Be aggressive for once. Don't hedge it around with qualifications. Don't get some hedger to write a dead introduction saying, "On the one hand, we have the evidence . . . on the other, we know that ghosts don't exist, but isn't it fun all the same." Back it with everything, print as many supporting letters as you can get, and tell them all – all the writers and critics and academics – that this book will change (*a*) what they're researching into (*b*) what they think about literature (*c*) what they think about life. Bash into them all, and it'll go like a bomb.'

'Not your usual measured tone, Philip,' said MacMichael.

'No, but this isn't your usual book. I'd even be prepared to put some of my own money into it.'

'Out of the question,' said MacMichael, 'it must be a collective decision, rationally arrived at.'

'There's one thing, Philip,' (Fazan this time, with a dangerously facetious intonation) 'what about copyright?'

'No problem there, surely,' put in Rollitt, speaking for the first time. 'As far as Mrs. Beesley's copyright goes, it's plain sailing. As for the ghosts, we win either way. If a ghost can't have copyright, we're in the clear. If one of their descendents fights it and wins, it means that courts, as well as the academic world, will be seen to endorse the fact that these texts are genuine and original pieces of writing.'

It was neat. 'And if they do fight,' I added, 'it's all the more publicity.'

My fellow-directors were, I suspected, intrigued by the idea of a scholarly press producing a collection of communications from the spirit-world. Intrigued as you might be at seeing a man in a three-piece suit roller-skating down St. James's. But would one *really* consider doing it oneself? It was time to give them something to back up their fancy.

'I've duplicated all the texts for you to study, and all the replies we've had so far, including the lukewarm ones. I've also written a report explaining the background to each text, where it fits in to the writer's work, what its relevance is. It's only an amateur report, and I'm sure there are mistakes; but it'll give you a line on what could be done by way of presentation, if we could get a real scholar to do it for us.'

The meeting adjourned; it had gone somewhat better than I had expected.

The following Friday Robert and I were back at Sherwin Mansions for the first time since Ellen Beesley had returned from hospital. The preliminary tests had disclosed nothing of significance, and the results of more speculative attempts to find out what was wrong would not now come in for a few days. Ellen explained, with her usual precision, 'It's quite straightforward. I'm perfectly healthy in one way. There's nothing, as they say, organically wrong. It's merely that I suffer from regular bouts of extreme pain which are gradually increasing in severity.'

'Well, I don't think you'd better be at your desk tonight, my dear,' said William.

'On the contrary,' she replied. 'I'm not going on any sea cruises. I'm not going to behave like an invalid. Most of all, I'm not giving up my Friday evenings.'

That, it was clear, was that; and I can't say that I was anything but relieved. We had not yet, in my opinion, assembled quite enough material to make the book the right length. If it was too short, it would be dismissed as 'a humorous trifle,' 'a squib,' 'a slender fantasy'; and in any case, we should have to take care not to publish anywhere near April 1st, or Christmas. If it was too long, it would qualify for 'extended fantasy' (which few will buy) or (worst of all) 'tireless imagination'. No, a nice, neat, 176-pager with the price creeping into the general-market range, was what I wanted.

Tonight, to my commercial and personal satisfaction, Ellen was kept extremely busy. Promptly at seven the first spirit arrived, and there were only brief pauses between visitors. Up there in the ether, the ghosts were clearly stacking like planes approaching Kennedy. Precisely at eight, though, Ellen's pen stopped in her hand, in mid-sentence.

This time, as I leafed through the dozen or so communications, I began to notice a new, and more disorientating note. There were, as usual, a couple in which the past annotated the past; and a few of the sort which had initially startled me, in which the past commented on its future, our present (this time, one from T. S. Eliot, a matronly castigation of the biographies of him published since his death). But in several of them, there was something new.

'Listen,' I said. 'It's Robert Bridges: "the appointment of J. W. Mallard as Poet Laureate in succession to Sir John Betjeman, though rightly attracting the scorn of the cartoonists, has, to a former incumbent of the Royal position, a more serious aspect . . ." '

'Christ,' said Robert. 'The future as well.'

'I suppose there's no logical reason why not,' commented Ellen. 'We must just all learn to be less proprietorial about the present.'

There were several other – prophecies, I was going to say, except that they treated the future as something that had already happened. And then there was a new turn. I picked up another page. It was headed: 'Dr. Leavis and Mr. D. H. Lawrence: A Reply'.

'And what about *this*?'

'Christ,' said Robert again, 'what does that mean?'

'Well, it must mean that Leavis's spirit has picked up what Lawrence sent us some weeks back,' said William.

'But Leavis isn't dead.'

'Indeed not.'

'Unless he got hold of the Lawrence piece somehow,' said Robert. 'Who did you send it out to, Philip?'

I consulted my file. 'That was one of the ones I didn't send out.'

'So it must mean,' went on Robert, 'that the spirit-world is not just something we attain after death, but something we are constantly present in, without our knowledge, all the time we're alive?'

'You'll make an orthodox Christian yet,' I said with a laugh.

'But it's a perfectly logical situation, isn't it,' said Ellen. 'If we posit a spirit-world which lacks our concept of time, why should existence in that world be dependent on an event rooted in time as understood in this world? In fact, doesn't this explain those names we couldn't identify, and which William couldn't trace in either the *D.N.B.* or the British Museum catalogue? Couldn't they be names from the future, or names of people alive now who haven't written anything?'

'It is all pretty logical, in a way,' said Robert.

'I'm not sure, though, if that's too much of a recommendation,' continued Ellen. 'After all, if our sense of time is irrelevant to the other world, why should our sense of logic be a trustworthy guide either?'

I was beginning to wonder why so many of her statements ended in questions, when the glass of water suddenly struck the carpet at my feet. I looked up, and saw that her eyes were closed, her teeth hard together, her back arching forwards, and her hands splayed out against the sides of the chair. She uttered no sound as William and Robert picked her up and carried her to the bedroom.

'Do you think there's any connection?' I asked, as Robert and I were making our way out.

'What, with the writing? Indirectly, I suppose. She's a very sensitive woman. If she can experience spirits, she can probably experience pain more than we can too.'

'Yes, of course; but what I meant was, do you think the spirits are doing this to her? If they can move her hand and arm, presumably they can affect all her nerve-endings.'

'Why should they? What would be their motive? I mean, what does it look like? It looks like back pain.'

'Well, it looks like unexplained back pain.'

'Yes.'

'Robert, would it be a fanciful suggestion ... I mean, could it be more than a metaphor ... but if, say, the spirits of the past wanted to attack a person, what part of them would be turned towards the spirits and open to attack?'

'You are being fanciful. And over-metaphorical. And you're forgetting that we've now got spirits of the present and future knocking around as well.'

'But the past might fear for its secrets more than the future.'

'I should expect it to be the other way round, if anything.'
'Yes, I suppose so.'

The next L.U.P. meeting went even better than I had hoped. Hirsh's letter was obviously a key factor. Purdy and Rollitt professed themselves enthusiastic about the whole project. Fazan had been clearly impressed by the academic testimonials. Even MacMichael, the chairman, cautiously agreed that we should push ahead. This surprised me, as I had been fearing some unpredictable action on his part; but for the moment, anyway, I was content with things.

We decided to send out more manuscripts, this time not just of the safe sort; and to sound out the academics who had responded favourably to my first letter about the possibility of publishing their replies. We agreed that we would try to make the most of Professor Hirsh's enthusiasm by laying before him all the facts of the case and inviting him to write an introduction and notes. His presence coupled with our imprint would, we hoped, ensure a serious reception for the book.

After the meeting I rang the Beesleys to tell them the progress that had been made. William received the news with little enthusiasm. Ellen, it appeared, had suffered a series of attacks, and was now under heavy sedation. The doctors and specialists were as puzzled as before. Tentatively, I outlined to William what I had said to Robert the night before.

'I don't think that's very likely,' he said. 'It's probably just the strain and excitement.'

'Did she ever have any attacks before she began this writing?'

'No, I don't think so.'

'Well then, isn't it obvious that there's some connection – that the spirits want to guard their secrets, for instance?'

'Why assume that the spirits are malevolent, Philip? And anyway, if they wanted to keep their secrets, then they don't have to communicate, do they?'

'Maybe they can't help it. Or maybe the ones who aren't communicating are trying to stop the ones who are.'

'Well, what evidence is there for that?'

'None, I suppose. Look, why don't we shelve the whole thing for a while. Get Ellen to stop her Fridays, and I'll soft-pedal on the publication side of it.'

'Absolutely not, Philip, absolutely not. Ellen and I have discussed this very point, and she's adamant. Her Fridays must continue.'

I paused. 'What if it kills her?'

Surprisingly, he didn't try to laugh it off. 'It's a risk that she's willing to take.'

Late the next Friday afternoon, I was in my office when MacMichael put his head round the door. 'Just been on the phone to New York,' he said. 'Quite by chance, actually. I'm afraid they told me that, as it happens, Hirsh has just died.'

'Bloody hell.'

'Yes. Quite unexpected, apparently. Heart attack. I shouldn't think he even got our letter. I've ... suggested to the other directors that we should meet – perhaps in half an hour?'

'Yes, sure.' It was the worst thing that could have happened; even worse, I realized, than if Ellen died. Typical of MacMichael, too, to call a meeting right at the end of Friday, when enthusiasm for continuing shaky prospects was bound to be at its lowest. The meeting was protracted and, mainly as a result of my attitude, rather bad-tempered. But the result was never in doubt. Hirsh had, after all, been the clinching factor in the decision to publish; his reputation would have carried the book if our integrity had been impugned; and who could I offer from my list of correspondents who was of comparable status? In short, the whole scheme should be – well, perhaps not dropped – but shelved, anyway. Indefinitely, was the implication.

By the time the meeting was over it was well after six.

I dashed across London to Sherwin Mansions as fast as I could, and hurried into that strange hothouse for what I thought might be the last time. I was eager to persuade Ellen that it would be pointless, for a while, to risk taxing her health any further. William answered the door with a long face and a finger to his lips.

'Ellen's just started,' he whispered.

I followed him softly into the sitting-room, raised a palm to Robert who was crouching in an arm-chair, and sat down to watch Ellen. Her hand raced across the paper as I sat going over the events of the last few months. I was in the process of being uncharitable about MacMichael when Robert's voice interrupted. 'Philip, this one seems to be for you . . .' He had picked up the top paper from Ellen's desk and was passing it over. I read:

University of Princeton,
Princeton, New Jersey 08540.
March 15th, 1974.

Dear Mr. Euchre,

Thank you for your letter of March 7th and the extraordinary revelations it contained. I must say that I have always considered the whole question of the existence of a spirit world and its ability to communicate with the living world to be a matter of interest only to the profoundly gullible. However, in the light of what you say . . .

DENGUÉ FEVER

by Paul Theroux

THERE is a curious tree, native to Malaysia, called 'The Midnight Horror'. We had several in Ayer Hitam, one in an overgrown part of the Botanical Gardens, the other in the front garden of William Ladysmith's house. His house was huge, nearly as grand as mine, but I was the American Consul and Ladysmith was an English teacher on a short contract. I assumed it was the tree that had brought the value of his house down. The house itself had been built before the war – one of those great breezy places, a masterpiece of colonial carpentry, with cement walls two feet thick and window blinds the size of sails on a Chinese junk. It was said that it had been the centre of operations during the occupation. All this history diminished by a tree! In fact, no local person would go near the house; the Chinese members of the staff at Ladysmith's school chose to live in that row of low warrens near the bus depot.

During the day the tree looked comic, a tall simple pole like an enormous coat-rack, with big leaves that looked like branches – but there were very few of them. It was covered with knobs, stark black things; and around the base of the trunk there were always fragments of leaves that looked like shattered bones, but not human bones.

At night the tree was different, not comic at all. It was Ladysmith who showed me the underlined passage in his copy of Professor Corner's *Wayside Trees of Malaya.* Below the entry for *Oroxylum indicum* it read, 'Botanically, it is the sole representative of its kind, aesthetically, it is monstrous . . . The corolla begins to open about ten p.m., when the tumid, wrinkled lips part and the harsh odour escapes from them. By midnight, the lurid mouth gapes widely and is filled with stink . . . The flowers are pollinated by bats which are attracted by the smell and, holding to the fleshy corolla with the claws on their wings, thrust their noses into its throat; scratches, as of bats, can be seen on the fallen leaves the next morning . . .'

Smelly! Ugly! Pollinated by bats! I said, 'No wonder no one wants to live in this house.'

'It suits me fine,' said Ladysmith. He was a lanky fellow, very pleasant, one of our uncomplicated Americans, who thrives in bush postings. He cycled around in his Bermuda shorts, organizing talent shows in *kampongs*. His description in my consulate file was 'Low risk, high gain'. Full of enthusiasm and blue-eyed belief; and open-hearted: he was forever having tea with tradesmen, whose status was raised as soon as he crossed the threshold.

Ladysmith didn't come round to the club much, although he was a member and had appeared in the Footlighters' production of Maugham's *The Letter*. I think he disapproved of us. He was young, one of the Vietnam generation with a punished conscience and muddled notions of colonialism. That war created drop-outs, but Ladysmith I took to be one of the more constructive ones, a volunteer teacher. After the cease-fire there were fewer; now there are none, neither hippies nor do-gooders. Ladysmith was delighted to take his guilt to Malaysia, and he once told me that Ayer Hitam was more lively than his home town, which surprised me until he said he was from Caribou, Maine.

He was tremendously popular with his students. He had put up a backboard and basketball hoop in the playground and after school he taught them the fundamentals of the game. He was, for all his apparent awkwardness, an athletic fellow, though it didn't show until he was in action – jumping or dribbling a ball down the court. Perhaps it never does. He ate like a horse, and knowing he lived alone I made a point of inviting him often to dinners for visiting firemen from Kuala Lumpur or Singapore. He didn't have a cook; he said he would not have a servant, but I don't believe he would have got any local person to live in his house, so close to that grotesque tree.

I was sorry but not surprised, two months after he arrived, to hear that Ladysmith had a fever, Ayer Hitam was malarial, and the tablets we took every Sunday like communion were only suppressants. The Chinese headmaster at the school stopped in at the consulate and said that Ladysmith wanted to see me. I went that afternoon.

The house was empty; a few chairs in the sitting-room, a shelf of paperbacks, a short-wave radio, and in the room beyond, a table holding only a large bottle of ketchup. The kitchen smelled of peanut butter and stale bread. Bachelor's quarters. I climbed the stairs, but before I entered the bedroom I heard Ladysmith call out in an anxious voice, 'Who is it?'

'Boy, am I glad to see you,' he said, relaxing as I came through the door.

He looked thinner, his face grey, his hair awry in bunches of standing hackles; and he lay in the rumpled bed as if he had been thrown there. His eyes were sunken and oddly coloured with the yellow light of fever.

'Malaria?'

'I think so – I've been taking chloroquine. But it doesn't seem to be working. I've got the most awful headache.' He closed his eyes. 'I can't sleep. I have these nightmares. I—'

'What does the doctor say?'

'I'm treating myself,' said Ladysmith.

'You'll kill yourself,' I said. 'I'll send Alec over tonight.'

We talked for a while, and eventually I convinced Ladysmith that he needed attention. Alec Stewart was a member of the club Ladysmith particularly disliked. He wasn't a bad sort, but as he was married to a Chinese girl he felt he could call them 'Chinks' without blame. He had been a ship's surgeon in the Royal Navy and had come to Ayer Hitam after the war. With a young wife and all that sunshine he was able to reclaim some of his youth. Back at the office I sent my *peon* Peeraswami over with a pot of soup and the latest issue of *Newsweek* from the consulate library.

Alec went that night. I saw him at the club later. He said, 'Our friend's pretty rocky.'

'I had malaria myself,' I said. 'It wasn't much fun.'

Alec blew a cautionary snort. 'He's not got malaria. He's got dengué.'

'Are you sure?'

'All the symptoms are there.'

'What did you give him for it?'

'The only thing there is worth a docken – aspirin.'

'I'll suppose he'll have to sweat it out.'

'He'll do that all right.' Alex leaned over. 'The lad's having hallucinations.'

'I didn't know that was a symptom of dengué,' I said.

'Dengué's a curse.'

He described it to me. It is a virus, carried by a mosquito, and begins as a headache of such voltage that you tremble and can't stand or sit. You're knocked flat; your muscles ache, you're doubled up with cramp and your temperature stays over a hundred. Then your skin becomes paper-thin, sensitive to the slightest touch – the weight of a sheet can cause pain. And your hair falls out – not all of it, but enough to fill a comb. These severe irritations produce another agony, a depression so black the dengué sufferer continually sobs. All the while your bones ache, as if every inch of you has been smashed with a hammer. This sensation of bruising gives dengué its colloquial name, 'break-bone fever'. I pitied Ladysmith.

Although it was after eleven when Alec left the club, I went straight over to Ladysmith's house. I was walking up the gravel drive when I heard the most ungodly shriek – frightening in its intensity and full of alarm. I did not recognize it as Ladysmith's – indeed, it scarcely sounded human. But it was coming from his room. It was so loud and changed in pitch with such suddenness it might easily have been two or three people screaming, or a dozen doomed cats. The Midnight Horror tree was in full bloom and filled the night with stink.

Ladysmith lay in bed whimpering. The magazine I'd sent him was tossed against the wall, and the effect of disorder was heightened by the overhead fan, which was lifting and ruffling the pages.

He was propped on one arm, but seeing me he sighed and fell back. His face was slick with perspiration and tear-streaks. He was short of breath.

'Are you all right?'

'My skin is burning,' he said. I noticed his lips were swollen and cracked with fever, and I saw then how dengué was like a species of grief.

'I thought I heard a scream,' I said. Screaming takes energy; Ladysmith was beyond screaming.

'Massacre,' he said. 'Soldiers – killing women and children. Horrible. Over there—' he pointed to a perfectly ordinary table with a jug of water on it, and he breathed, 'War. You should see their faces, all covered with blood. Some have arms missing. I've never—' He broke off and began to sob.

'Alec says you have dengué fever,' I said.

'Two of them – women. They look the same,' said Ladysmith lifting his head. 'They scream at me, and it's so loud! They have no teeth!'

'Are you taking the aspirin?' I saw the amber jar was full.

'Aspirin! For this!' He lay quietly, then said, 'I'll be all right. Sometimes it's nothing – just a high temperature. Then these Chinese . . . then I get these dreams.'

'About war?'

'Yes. Flashes.'

As gently as I could I said, 'You didn't want to go to Vietnam, did you?'

'No. Nobody wanted to go. I registered as a c.o.'

Hallucinations are replies. Peeraswami was always seeing

Tamil ghosts on his way home. They leaped from those green fountains by the road the Malays call *daun pontianak* – 'ghost leaf' – surprising him with plates of hot samosas or tureens of curry; not so much ghosts as ghostesses. I told him to eat something before setting out from home in the dark and he stopped seeing them. I took Ladysmith's visions of massacre to be replies to his conscientious objection. It is the draft dodger who speaks most graphically of war, not the soldier. Pacifists know all the atrocity stories.

But Ladysmith's hallucinations had odd highlights: the soldiers he saw weren't American. They were dark orientals in dirty undershirts, probably Vietcong, and mingled with the screams of the people with bloody faces was another sound, the creaking of bicycle seats. So there were two horrors – the massacre and these phantom cyclists. He was especially frightened by the two women with no teeth, who opened their mouths wide and screamed at him.

I said, 'Give it a few days.'

'I don't think I can take much more of this.'

'Listen,' I said. 'Dengué can depress you. You'll feel like giving up and going home – you might feel like hanging yourself. But take these aspirin and keep telling yourself – whenever you get these nightmares – it's dengué fever.'

'No teeth, and their gums are dripping with blood—'

His head dropped to the pillow, his eyes closed, and I remember thinking: everyone is fighting this war, everyone in the world. Poor Ladysmith was fighting hardest of all. Lying there he could have been bivouacked in the Central Highlands, haggard from a siege, his dengué a version of battle fatigue.

I left him sleeping and walked again through the echoing house. But the smell had penetrated to the house itself, the high thick stink of rotting corpses. It stung my eyes and I almost fainted with the force of it until, against the moon, I saw that blossoming coat-rack and the wheeling bats – The Midnight Horror.

'Rotting flesh,' Ladysmith said late the next afternoon. I tried not to smile. I had brought Alec along for a second look. Ladysmith began describing the smell, the mutilated people, the sound of bicycles and those Chinese women, the toothless ones. The victims had pleaded with him. Ladysmith looked wretched.

Alec said, 'How's your head?'

'It feels like it's going to explode.'

Alec nodded. 'Joints a bit stiff?'

'I can't move.'

'Dengué's curse.' Alec smiled: doctors so often do when their grim diagnosis is proved right.

'*I can't—*' Ladysmith started, then grimaced and continued in a softer tone. 'I can't sleep. If I could sleep I'd be all right. For God's sake give me something to make me sleep.'

Alec considered this.

'Can't you give him anything?' I asked.

'I've never prescribed a sleeping-pill in my life,' said Alec, 'and I'm not going to do so now. Young man, take my advice. Drink lots of liquid – you're dehydrating. You've got a severe fever. Don't underestimate it. It can be a killer. But I guarantee if you follow my instructions, get lots of bed-rest, take aspirin every four hours, you'll be right as ninepence.'

'My hair is falling out.'

Alec smiled – right again. 'Dengué,' he said. 'But you've still got plenty. When you've as little hair as I have you'll have something to complain about.'

Outside the house I said, 'That tree is the most malignant thing I've ever seen.'

Alec said, 'You're talking like a Chink.'

'Sure, it looks innocent enough now, with the sun shining on it. But have you smelled it at night?'

'I agree. A wee aromatic. Like a Bengali's fart.'

'If we cut it down I think Ladysmith would stop having his nightmares.'

'Don't be a fool. That tree's medicinal. The Malays use it for potions. It works – I use it myself.'

'Well, if it's so harmless why don't the Malays want to live in this house?'

'It's not been offered to a Malay. How many Malay teachers do you know? It's the Chinks won't live here – I don't have a clue why that's so, but I won't have you running down that tree. It's going to cure our friend.'

I stopped walking. 'What do you mean by that?'

Alec said, 'The aspirin – or rather, not the aspirin. I'm using native medicine. Those tablets are made from the bark of that tree – I wish it didn't have that shocking name.'

'You're giving him *that*?'

'Calm down, it'll do him a world of good,' Alec said brightly. 'Ask any witch-doctor.'

I slept badly myself that night, thinking of Alec's ridiculous cure – he had truly gone bush – but I was tied up all day with visa inquiries and it was not until the following evening that I got back to Ladysmith's. I was determined to take him away. I had aspirin at my house; I'd keep him away from Alec.

Downstairs, I called out and knocked as usual to warn him I'd come, and as usual there was no response from him. I entered the bedroom and saw him asleep, but uncovered. Perhaps the fever had passed: his face was dry. He did not look well, but then few people do when they're sound asleep – most take on the ghastly colour of illness. Then I saw that the amber bottle was empty – the 'aspirin' bottle.

I tried to feel his pulse. Impossible: I've never been able to feel a person's pulse, but his hand was cool, almost cold I put my ear against his mouth and thought I could detect a faint purr of respiration.

It was dusk when I arrived, but darkness in Ayer Hitam fell quickly, the blanket of night dropped and the only warning was the sound of insects tuning up, the chirrup of geckoes and those squeaking bats making for the tree. I switched on the lamp and as I did so heard a low cry, as of someone dying in dreadful pain. And there by the window – just as Ladysmith had described – I saw the moonlit faces of two Chinese women, smeared with blood. They opened their mouths and howled; they were toothless and their screeches seemed to gain volume from that emptiness.

'Stop!' I shouted.

The two faces in those black rags hung there, and I caught the whiff of the tree which was the whiff of wounds. It should have scared me, but it only surprised me. Ladysmith had prepared me, and I felt certain that he had passed that horror on. I stepped forward, caught the cord and dropped the window blinds. The two faces were gone.

This took seconds, but an after-image remained, like a lamp switched rapidly on and off. I gathered up Ladysmith. Having lost weight he was very light, pathetically so. I carried him downstairs and through the garden to the road.

Behind me, in the darkness, was the rattle of pedals, the squeak of a bicycle seat. The phantom cyclists! It gave me a shock, and I tried to run, but carrying Ladysmith I could not move quickly. The cycling noises approached, frantic squeakings at my back. I spun round.

It was a trishaw, cruising for fares. I put Ladysmith on the seat, and running alongside it we made our way to the mission hospital.

A stomach pump is little more than a slender rubber tube pushed into one nostril and down the back of the throat. A primitive device: I couldn't watch. I stayed until Ladysmith regained consciousness. But it was useless to talk to him. His stomach was empty and he was coughing up bile, spewing into a bucket. I told the nursing sister to keep an eye on him.

I said, 'He's got dengué.'

The succeeding days showed such an improvement in Ladysmith that the doctors insisted he be discharged to make room for more serious cases. And indeed everyone said he'd made a rapid recovery. Alec was astonished, but told him rather sternly, 'You should be ashamed of yourself for taking that overdose.'

Ladysmith was well, but I didn't have the heart to send him back to that empty house. I put him up at my place. Normally, I hated house-guests – they interfered with my reading and never seemed to have much to do themselves except punish my gin bottle. But Ladysmith was unobtrusive. He drank milk, he wrote letters home. He made no mention of his hallucinations, and I didn't tell him what I'd thought I'd seen. In my own case I believe his suggestions had been so strong that I had imagined what he had seen – somehow shared his own terror of the toothless women.

One day at lunch Ladysmith said, 'How about eating out tonight? On me. A little celebration. After all, you saved my life.'

'Do you feel well enough to face the club buffet?'

He made a face. 'I hate the club – no offence. But I was thinking of a meal in town. What about that *kedai* – City Bar? I had a terrific meal there the week I arrived. I've been meaning to go back.'

'You're the boss.'

It was a hot night. The verandah tables were taken, so we had to sit inside, jammed against a wall. We ordered: mee-hoon soup, spring rolls, pork strips, fried kway-teow and a bowl of laksa that seemed to blister the lining of my mouth.

'One thing's for sure,' said Ladysmith, 'I won't get dengué fever again for a while. The sister said I'm immune for a year.'

'Thank God for that,' I said. 'By then you'll be back in Caribou, Maine.'

'I don't know,' he said. 'I like it here.'

He was smiling, glancing around the room, poking noodles into his mouth. Then I saw him lose control of his chopsticks. His jaw dropped, he turned pale, and I thought for a moment that he was going to cry.

'Is anything wrong?'

He shook his head, but he looked stricken.

'It's this food,' I said. 'You shouldn't be eating such strong—'

'No,' he said. 'It's those pictures.'

On the white-washed wall of the *kedai* was a series of framed photographs, old hand-coloured ones, lozenge-shaped, like huge lockets. Two women and some children. Not so unusual; the Chinese always have photographs of relations around – a casual reverence. One could hardly call them a pious people; their brand of religion is ancestor worship, the simple display of the family album. But I had not realized until then that Woo Boh Swee's relations had had money. The evidence was in the pictures: both women were smiling, showing large sets of gold dentures.

'That's them,' said Ladysmith.

'Who?' I said. Staring at them I noticed certain wrinkles of familiarity, but the Chinese are very hard to tell apart. The cliché is annoyingly true.

Ladysmith put his chopsticks down and began to whisper: 'The women in my room – that's *them.* That one had blood on her hair, and the other one—'

'Dengué fever,' I said. 'You said they didn't have any teeth. Now I ask you – look at those teeth. You've got the wrong ladies, my boy.'

'No!'

His pallor had returned, and the face I saw across the table was the one I had seen on that pillow. I felt sorry for him, as helpless as I had before.

Woo Boh Swee, the owner of City Bar, went by the table. He was brisk, snapping a towel. 'Okay? Anything? More beer? What you want?'

'We're fine, Mr. Woo,' I said. 'But I wonder if you can tell us something. We were wondering who those women are in the pictures – over there.'

He looked at the wall, grunted, lowered his head and simply walked away, muttering.

'I don't get it,' I said. I left the table and went to the back of the bar, where Boh Swee's son Reggie – the 'English' son

– was playing mah-jongg. I asked Reggie the same question: who are they?

'I'm glad you asked me,' said Reggie. 'Don't mention them to my father. One's his auntie, the other one's his sister. It's a sad story. They were cut up during the war by the dwarf bandits. That's what my old man calls them in Hokkien. The Japanese. It happened over at the headquarters – what they used for headquarters when they occupied the town. My old man was in Singapore.'

'But the Japanese were only here for a few months,' I said.

'Bunch of thieves,' said Reggie. 'They took anything they could lay their hands on. They used those old ladies for house-girls, at the headquarters, that big house, where the tree is. Then they killed them, just like that, and hid the bodies – we never found the graves. But that was before they captured Singapore. The British couldn't stop them, you know. The dwarf bandits were clever – they pretended they were Chinese and rode all the way to the Causeway on bicycles.'

I looked back at the table. Ladysmith was staring, his eyes again bright with fever; staring at those gold teeth.

THE SWORD OF FREY

by Brian R. Hall

My father was imprisoned in Stalag XXIVB for four years, but it was not until the year after his death, when I found his diaries, that I understood his reluctance to speak about Von Beckdorf, the camp commandant, and his absolute refusal to explain or even to speculate upon the man's disappearance.

Von Beckdorf came from an old Prussian family connected to the Swedish nobility, and had been educated in England. His English was faultless, and he affected the manners and pursuits of an English gentleman, dressing in tweeds and maintaining his London accounts through neutral intermediaries. As a man, he despised Hitler and the Nazis, yet he could see no other course for Germany.

My father was an inveterate diarist, and it has been necessary to cut out a great deal, in order to arrive at the details of how the Sword came into his possession, and how Von Beckdorf vanished from the earth. The first entry dates from his arrival at the prison camp.

We were a curious rabble at the transit camp. Few of us had any kit, and my only extra consisted of a double-lined British Warm, equipped with poacher's pockets. For some reason, I had taken to keeping my personal diaries in these pockets, and the search being less than thorough they were never discovered.

Shortly after dawn on the second day of capture, we were roughly sorted into groups of thirty or so, and herded into open trucks. There were no seats, and most preferred to stand and hang on to the sides. We travelled all day, with no stops for food or water, and must have crossed the German border just after dark. The trucks stopped in a village, and Wermacht officers went from lorry to lorry, calling out names and packing their owners off into the darkness. Before long, a large figure in a long grey coat approached the lorry in which I was standing.

'Major Stewart?' he asked, looking up. I saw that he was a warrant officer, and that unlike his higher-ranking colleagues he was dressed in a most exact fashion, his leather gleaming as if it had been newly polished. I later discovered that it had.

I identified myself, and the figure saluted with absolute correctness.

'Oberfeldwebel Gerber,' he said, his heels clicking. 'You will accompany me please.' Then, as if he had forgotten himself, he made a gesture of apology.

'Your luggage, Major?' he asked.

'Luggage?' I replied, stupidly. 'Of course not. I'm a prisoner of war!'

'We will send for whatever you need,' he said, with some disapproval, and, letting in the clutch of the military Volkswagen to which we had transferred, drove away from the village.

We had been travelling for perhaps an hour when the lights of another village showed through the pine-trees. The Volkswagen turned abruptly, and we climbed through shrubs and more pines, suddenly debouching on to a gravel drive in front of what in England would have been a substantial country house. On the steps, beneath flickering pine torches set in iron brackets, stood a tall, good-looking man in whipcord breeches, leather jacket, and tall polished boots.

Gerber leaped from the car with an agility surprising in one so bulky, and opened my door with a flourish, saluting and clicking his heels at the same time.

'Major Stewart!' he announced.

'Von Beckdorf,' said the tall man, coming forward with outstretched hand. 'I am delighted to see you. Welcome to Schiffhausen. I'm sorry for the circumstances in which we meet, but I hope our hospitality will go some way to make up for that. Come along, Gerber will show you to your room, then we'll have dinner.'

Dazed, I followed Gerber up the polished pine stairs to a large bedroom where, despite the unseasonably warm weather, a log fire was burning. Gerber drew the curtains, and showed me a small but functional bathroom. Then, saluting again, he withdrew. As the door closed softly behind him, I heard the unmistakable sound of a large key turning in the lock. Swiftly, I inspected the room. It would have been a simple matter for a professional escaper to find a way out, but to my inexperienced eye it looked impossibly prison-like. Above and below me were other rooms, and the bathroom had no window. The single window in the bedroom, though large, was heavily barred, and the room had probably been a nursery.

It took me a second or two to recognize Gerber when he next opened the door. He had changed from his Wermacht field-grey to the uniform of a butler, the black coat and trousers suiting him just as well as the military garb.

'The Count awaits you, sir,' he said, and indicated that I should follow him. I don't know why I should have imagined that Von Beckdorf and I would be eating alone, but I was conducted into a small room, where there were at least two other British officers, an American, and a Belgian pilot.

'Major Stewart,' said Von Beckdorf. 'I hope you are feeling rested? What can I offer you to drink? We have almost anything you care to name, I think. We took care to stock our cellars before the war.' He then introduced me to my fellow prisoners, though they hardly seemed that.

I had been in bed ten minutes, comfortably aware of an excellent meal, when I heard the key in the door, followed by a knock. Upon my call, Von Beckdorf entered and switched on the main light.

'My dear Stewart,' he said, an embarrassed expression on his face. 'I am truly sorry to disturb you, but I make a point of getting through official business as quickly as possible. It helps to do it discreetly, you know.' Opening a folder, he asked me those questions which I was permitted to answer, and no others.

'Now,' he said, closing the folder. 'The unofficial questions.' Then, seeing my expression, he laughed. 'Domestic matters, Major. Not military. I wish to ensure that you are as comfortable as possible.'

A fortnight passed in this extraordinary manner, the few prisoners in the house meeting only at mealtimes. In the event, despite my long stay at Schiffhausen, I exchanged only pleasantries with them, and in two cases, never even knew their names. But Von Beckdorf saw me at some time every day, and I began to feel that he was making me into some kind of special prisoner.

As winter drew in, and the first snows fell, the atmosphere in the house changed. Gerber took to carrying out his duties in uniform, and the various male servants about the place suddenly appeared in field grey. As November drew to its close, Von Beckdorf could be seen inspecting the day's mail with a preoccupied air, and glancing apprehensively at each car or van which arrived. At length, that which he had been expecting, arrived. He announced the news at dinner.

'Gentlemen,' he began. 'I had hoped that the not inconsiderable influence which I still have in Germany would have protected my estates from interference. But I was wrong. We are to receive a visit from the Inspectorate tomorrow morning.' He paused, considering his next words.

'I need hardly tell you that this is a most unusual prison camp. Unfortunately, that is likely to be the opinion of our visitors. There is a possibility that you will be moved elsewhere, or that at the very least, your privileges will be restricted.'

He then changed the subject, and would not allow any of us to raise the matter again. The next day we were awakened at six by an anxious Gerber. Accustomed to a leisurely breakfast, we were astonished to be herded on to the front drive and formed into two ranks. We waited in the snow for perhaps one minute. Then Von Beckdorf appeared. He was dressed as a Colonel, and the uniform seemed to give him a dimension beyond that of the courteous jailer.

'Gentlemen!' he barked, his voice hard in the frosty half-light. 'The Inspectorate arrive in two hours. Oberfeldwebel Gerber will conduct you to temporary quarters.'

The temporary quarters, rough though they were, were quite sufficient. The Inspectorate, hard-faced men with clip-boards and suspicious eyes, watched us working, eating, sleeping, dressing and resting. That they were unsatisfied became obvious the day after they left. We were marched to the house and allowed back to our original rooms.

'It seems, gentlemen,' Von Beckdorf announced at our first meal in the house, 'that the Inspectorate consider you have been having an easy time. They have allocated you to other camps within the Reich. This Stalag will remain, as a temporary interrogation camp for important officers of the rank of Brigadier and above. I have been permitted to choose one officer to remain as my prisoner to act as, shall we say, personal liaison between myself and my future guests? That is a concession to me, personally.'

There was a long pause, while each of us, however much he would have liked to escape and rejoin his country's forces, secretly hoped that he would be chosen.

'I am sure you will not take it personally when you realize that you have not been chosen to remain behind. I should tell you, therefore, that I have chosen Major Stewart.'

My father remained at Schiffhausen for another three years. A few high-ranking officers came and went, but none of them impressed sufficiently to figure in his diaries.

Much of the last diary is written with an ersatz ink, as supplies were hard to come by in 1945, and I suspect that my father made it himself from oak galls gathered in the small patches of deciduous forest. With no stabilizing agents, much of the ink has faded, and in places the handwriting is such that it might have been written by a stranger. But I have transliterated those parts I can read, beginning with the day in April when my father and Von Beckdorf were sitting together after dinner, there being no prisoners to entertain.

I noticed Otto's face wore a curiously excited look, as if some great event were about to occur. Yet beneath there was strain, and a feverish kind of uncertainty.

'Douglas,' he began, for we had been on first name terms in private for a year or so. 'I am very much alone.'

I didn't know what he meant. But instead of further explanations, he got up from the table, motioning me to follow. Gerber came after, extracting a ring of keys. I followed Otto through the kitchen quarters, down to the wine-cellar. Gerber locked the door behind us and stood in the shadows, silent and watchful.

Otto gripped my hands and stared into my face.

'I am compelled to do – a certain thing,' he said. 'Every generation of Von Beckdorfs has to fight this compulsion, and I am weak. I don't think I can withstand it. But I need your help, as a friend.'

I didn't understand what he was talking about, and said so. But he took no notice of me, and stared into the shadows. I followed his gaze, and noticed the outline of a heavy, studded door. He stared at this for another minute, and then began to talk again in a near-normal voice.

'This house was built at the end of the seventeenth century, on the ruins of a much older house. This cellar, and the lower cellars, date from that earlier house. In 1560, a Von Beckdorf was serving as a mercenary officer in the armies of Charles V, and he saved the Emperor's life at some minor skirmish. It seems the Emperor decided that this act was worthy of the highest honour, and he presented my ancestor with a sword from his treasure, one which was never used by any man, and was said to have been the property of Frodi, King of the Danes at the time of Christ. Now, I don't know how much you know of our ancient myths, but it is said that this sword was forged by dwarves for the god Frey in that time when there were giants and men were animals.'

My expression must have shown my opinion of this portentous nonsense, for Otto grasped my hands again.

'Listen,' he cried. 'I don't know whether the story is true or not. But I do know this. Von Beckdorf was a soldier of considerable ability. He took little note of superstitions, and when the tale was told to him by one of the Emperor's secretaries, he laughed until the tears rolled down his cheeks. He made a point of using that sword in the following battle. It is said that he killed four hundred and twenty men that day, and both armies feared him, for the common soldiers said that the sword fought alone, beyond the reach of his hand, and yet dragged him about with it until those able to had fled the field. Then he sheathed the sword. After that, he gave up war and came here, to Schiffhausen. He built a shaft in the deepest cellar, down which he thrust the sword, and placed a heavy stone above it. That stone is now the centre of the cellar beneath us.'

The silence grew oppressive, and I could hear Gerber breathing. Otto's grip upon my hands hadn't slackened, and his gaze grew more intense. I felt a chill across the base of my neck, as if the temperature had suddenly dropped, and fought within myself an unreasoning fear of what might lie in that lower cellar.

'You expect me to believe,' I asked, trying to keep my voice steady, 'that the sword still lies beneath that stone? Why man, even if it does, it'll be no more than rust! Here we are, discussing some mythical sword and the antics of your ancestors while Europe collapses above our heads!'

Otto van Beckdorf still stared at me. He did not appear to have heard a single word I said. Abruptly, he let go of my hands. Walking to the studded door, he took down from a hook a massive iron key, which he threw at my feet.

'There!' he shouted. 'That key hasn't been used by a Von Beckdorf since 1811! By my great-great-grandfather. He was a drunk. One night he took a few of his drinking friends down to that cellar. They lifted the stone, and my ancestor reached down for the sword. Taking it from the pit, he waved it in the air, and said that no Von Beckdorf worthy of the name believed such rubbish, and no Von Beckdorf ever would!'

'What happened?' I asked, fascinated, despite myself.

Otto sat on an old wine-cask, and motioned to Gerber, who brought him a bottle of brandy and a glass. His face was even more drawn than before, and his hands trembled.

'Not a soul left that cellar,' he said. 'He took the sword from the scabbard, made a few imaginary passes with it, and within seconds there were six men dead upon the floor. The sword waited, almost as if thinking, then twisted in his hand, and with one colossal stroke, sliced through his neck.'

'There isn't much more,' he added. 'A servant had been waiting at the head of the steps, saw it all, and slammed and locked the door. He claimed after that he heard the blade slide back into the scabbard, and the grating of stone on stone. But there hasn't been a Von Beckdorf since who hasn't believed that tale implicitly, and not one who has been in that cellar again.'

'Do you mean,' I asked, 'the bodies have been there ever since 1811? My God, what sort of superstitious people are you? Come on, give me the key! I'll soon show you what sort of rubbish this is!'

But Gerber moved from the shadows to stand between me and the door.

Otto laughed, though there was no humour in it.

'This won't take long,' he said, and nodded to Gerber, who gave me a warning glance, as if to tell me not to attempt the door. He went into a small store room and at length emerged, carrying a most extraordinary contraption. It appeared to be some sort of animal trap, but its sheer strength and massive construction made that unlikely.

'Look,' said Otto. 'As far as I know, this cage is sufficiently long to hold the sword in its scabbard.'

'If the sword hasn't been seen for as long as you say,' I asked, 'how can you possibly know?'

'I've known about this cage since I was a child,' he said. 'My father had it made. There are treasury inventories of Charles V in Paris, and one of them gives the dimensions of the sword.'

'But if it were possible to approach it so closely then,' I argued, 'why not now? Why should it suddenly spring to life again like this?'

'Because it has tasted blood twice, in the hands of this family.'

'Assuming everything you've said to be true,' I said. 'Why wouldn't it turn on me, and then you and your family?'

'Have you forgotten what my ancestor said?' he whispered. 'He said no Von Beckdorf would ever believe in the sword! Only a man who believes and is not afraid can hold it in his hand!'

Despite myself I felt Otto's conviction taking root in my mind. But despite that, I knew I had no choice, even if it were only a question of proving him wrong.

'Very well,' I said. 'Let's get this over. But . . .'

Otto held up his hand.

'No conditions. You must go into that cellar believing in the sword, and in me. You must promise to do what I've asked.'

We knelt by the cage while he pointed out various features, including heavy collars to go about the handle. The whole thing was made of high-quality steel, and I believe a tank could have driven over it without causing damage. No sword could get out once locked in there.

'Very well,' I said. 'I believe you.'

And I knew that the atmosphere was such that I did, despite what I might feel the next day. But Gerber? Did he believe? Would the sword turn and rend him? His expression made me bite back any comment I might have made. He was ready to follow and assist in whatever we had to do. He was a servant of the Von Beckdorfs.

Otto picked up the key and handed it to me.

'I'm going to the village,' he said. 'I will be gone in ten minutes. It would be safer if I were not here when the sword is brought out.'

I nodded agreement, and watched him go up the stairs to the kitchen. The ten minutes stretched on and on. At length, Gerber looked at his watch.

'It is time,' he said.

I inserted the key and turned. It moved more easily than I expected, but the door stayed firmly shut.

'Again,' said Gerber.

I turned the key once more, and heard a second bolt slide back. Placing both hands on the twisted iron handle, I pulled. With grinding hinges, the door swung open, releasing a puff of dry and musty air. I felt, foolishly, for a lightswitch before Gerber pushed a candle into my hand, lighting one for himself at the same time. The flames threw innumerable dark shadows down the stone steps. Beyond the light was an absolute blackness which only gradually retreated as we slowly descended. Soon, I could see the centre of the floor, and in the middle a massive stone, slightly above the level of its companions. As I moved the candle round, the light reflected back from small items on the floor. Brass candle-holders of an antique style. A coin. A ring.

And then, against the walls, the dusty brown of human bones. The clothes which had once been worn by those drinking men, so long ago, were hardly rotted, and lay just as they had fallen. The whole scene looked so calm and still that I was tempted to forget my promise to Otto. But Gerber pushed past me and bent down at the last step where something glimmered in the candle light. He picked it up and showed it to me without a word. It was a skull, the jaws jammed open in a rictus of death. From the depression at the base of the skull hung three vertebrae. They detached themselves as Gerber touched them, falling to the floor in a noiseless cloud of dust.

We stood, taking in the atmosphere of the place. It was

not evil, or even frightening. Merely – powerful. I wasn't scared, or even apprehensive.

We carried down the cage and some iron levers, and I opened the locks and set the combinations. We lifted the stone and slid it out of the way. The 'pit' proved to be a shaft in the earth, about two feet across. I couldn't see anything with the candles, so I sent Gerber for an electric torch. I could feel the temperature rising for some reason, and before Gerber returned I had removed my pullover and opened my shirt. Yet when I touched the stone floor I found it chill and cold.

Gerber handed me the torch and I shone it down the shaft. Instantly light reflected back, dazzling me. But I had seen the outline of an enormous sword, leaning against the side of the shaft, its hilt glittering with polished stones.

I gave Gerber the torch, and asked him to keep the beam above my head. Lying on my stomach I rolled my shirt-sleeve back and reached down. As soon as my hand entered the shaft I felt a curious vibration. I could feel the skin on my forearm being pulled taut, and the blood racing into my fingers. I attempted to withdraw, but my resistance only increased the force, and a low humming rose from the shaft, sending my mind racing into incoherent patterns. I could feel the pulses beating in my skull, and a mist rose behind my eyes. The tingling in my skin grew to a pain, and my hand was dragged further and further down until my head and shoulders were in the shaft. I grasped the opposite side of the shaft with my free hand and shouted to Gerber to hold me. He had anticipated me, and was now lying solidly across my legs. I could no longer feel the fingers of my right hand, but at that moment I involuntarily grasped the handle of the sword and cried out with the pain.

I must have passed out for a few moments, for when I opened my eyes, Gerber was pulling at my legs, dragging me from the shaft. I could feel my hand gripping the sword and tried to let go. As if it sensed my wish, the sword cooled and the humming died away.

Once more, I reached into the shaft. There was no compulsion this time, merely a comfortable warmth. I felt oddly pleased, as if I knew that the sword had accepted me, for the time being, at least.

I grasped it firmly and lifted. As it emerged I saw that the whole weapon seemed to carry no dust at all. Laying it on the floor, I studied it.

'Put it in the cage, Major,' said Gerber, his eyes wide. 'The cage!'

It seemed harmless enough, and I wanted to have a good look first. But Gerber grew more agitated, and I became aware that the sword was beginning to glow with a soft light, and that Gerber's face reflected only one thing – fear!

'It won't harm you,' I assured him. 'It's accepted me. I'll hold it while I examine the hilt, then we'll lock it away.' But he wouldn't accept my word, and backed away. I didn't want to scare him unnecessarily, so I opened the cage and slid the sword into the place prepared. Before locking the cage, I saw that the hilt was of a style of workmanship totally unknown to me, and quite unlike what one might have expected. I held the handle once more and gently tugged, merely to get some idea of the appearance of the blade. But the sword responded, and had I not had a firm grip on it, the blade would have ejected itself. As it was, at least six inches came into view. It was about four inches across at the shoulder, and down the centre ran a concave channel. The metal was quite undecorated, but I could see that it was a very high-quality carbon steel, pattern-welded. On the edges was an inlaid strip of some other metal, forming a cutting edge. That metal was so dark and dull as to be almost black, and as I reached my free hand forward to touch it, the nearest edge shimmered, so that I snatched my hand away. But I had miscalculated. A single drop of blood appeared on the edge of the blade, and as I inspected my thumb, a small gash, like that from a new razor blade, oozed another drop. I watched the drop on the blade, and then it shimmered and disappeared, almost as if it had been absorbed. Once more the low humming started, and it must have been that which restored me to my senses, for I slammed the blade into the scabbard and into the cage, snapping the locks as I did so. The humming died away and I became aware of Gerber tugging at my sleeve. His face was quite white and his hands were shaking. But he took one of the handles and between us we took the sword up to the wine-cellar.

'Where now?' I asked.

'The stables,' he gasped. 'You'll be able to remove it from there and take it to England. The Count will never know or need to know where it is.'

We left the sword in an unused part of the stables, locking the door. The next days passed as before, broken only by news bulletins, both English and German. It was from these that we learned how near the Allies were to Schiffhausen, and a day or two later we heard gunfire in the west.

The next entry makes it clear that a very different state of affairs obtained on the day before the Allies arrived. My father woke at three in the morning, certain that something was wrong. He lay awake for some time, but heard nothing. At length, unable to get back to sleep, he dressed and went downstairs. As all pretence at being a prison-camp had been abandoned he was able to let himself out of the house and cross the stable yard without being challenged. He waited outside the stables, listening, but he could still hear nothing. The moon, half hidden by slow and pallid clouds, gave just enough light to see by.

I stood hesitating for a moment, feeling a bit foolish. There seemed to be no good reason for my fears, and I was uncomfortably aware of the sword, lying only a few yards away. It would do no harm to unlock the door and have a quick look, just to satisfy myself.

I approached, feeling in my pocket for the key. It was not there. I paused, unsure of my next move. Then I heard a curious sound. It was metal chinking, half muffled, as if whoever or whatever was making the noise was trying to keep as quiet as possible. It was then that I became aware of another sound, below that of the metal, but quickly building up to such a pitch that I had to place my hands on my ears and press until my head hurt. Anything to keep out that awful, soaring, humming sound. I had recognized it at once. It was the sword!

The humming rose and rose, until it was almost a kind of primitive voice. I felt myself drawn closer and closer to the door. As I pressed against the heavy woodwork, I felt a slight movement, and realized that the door was open. I pushed gently, until it stood away from me. Within the stable was a flickering fiery glow, rising and falling. And under the awful noise I could hear slow, laboured breathing.

Standing back, I kicked open the door. It swung away with heavy reluctance, revealing what I had subconsciously feared. Otto von Beckdorf had somehow found the sword, and was even now opening the last lock. Within the cage the sword quivered and shook, its radiance eager and its humming that of some savage and bloodthirsty animal.

I took a step forward, intending to grab Otto by the shoulders and drag him away, but as I did so the noise and light grew to a crescendo, and as the last lock fell open the sword flew from its scabbard and hung, point up, radiating hatred and fire. I tried to call out, but no words left my mouth. I tried to move, but my feet were held to the floor.

The sword hung, while I stood, and Otto crouched. The blade slowly fell back from the hilt, until the whole weapon was at an angle to the floor. Hilt first, it advanced upon my friend. It reached a point some two feet from him and then, with delicate precision, the blade swung through an arc until, by the time the edge reached him, it was moving too fast for the eye to follow. I cannot describe exactly what happened then. The edge descended on his head and seemed to pass right through him, until the point and six inches of the blade were buried deep in his heart. The horrible tableau remained like that for at least two minutes.

Perhaps Otto was already dead. Perhaps he had died the moment his body took up that unnaturally still position. Whatever the facts, I know that I then saw Otto actually shrink! Gradually, his face became whiter and whiter, until it seemed almost transparent. Then the skin began to fold in upon itself, like some old glove, until nothing was left but a pile of clothes, covering something which had been the carcase of Count Otto von Beckdorf.

The sword withdrew, and hung point down, the blade a deep ruby-red, darkening to black. As I watched, the radiance vanished, and the sword sank lower and lower, until it fell upon the stable floor, satiated and cold.

The force which had bound me left, and I felt myself shaking so much that I had to go back out into the yard. As I recovered, I found my mind trying to reject that which it knew to be true. But I also knew that no one would ever believe me.

I have no idea how long I stayed in the yard. Eventually I returned and replaced the sword in the cage. It felt dull, dead, lifeless. I picked up Otto's clothes, unable to take them apart for fear of what I knew to be there. I buried them deep in the forest, covering the grave with leaves and stones.

The Americans arrived the following day, and in the confusion, no one ever suspected the fate of the Count. I persuaded the British liaison officer to let me find my own way to a British unit, which he allowed me to do, after questioning.

At this point, my father's narrative ends. Further diaries make no reference to the story, or to Germany.

Perhaps it is just as well that he is dead. Two days ago, I received a rather odd letter. It was signed 'Fritz von Beckdorf,' and was most beautifully typed on heavily engraved business paper. It began in a formal style, identifying the writer, and mentioning that he was coming to London shortly, on business, and that he would like to meet me. But the last paragraph was quite different.

'I understand from my late father's butler, Gerber, that your father removed to England some family property which rightly belongs here at Schiffhausen. I have no knowledge of the circumstances in which it was removed, but after thirty years I think it should now be returned. I will be grateful for an opportunity to inspect the item(s) in question, and arrange for their return.'

Is this the compulsion of the Von Beckdorfs, to see, to touch the sword? Is it the senile Gerber revenging himself for the loss of his master? Is it my imagination, or does the sword, safely locked in my gun-room, show signs of life? And what could 'their' return mean?

On re-reading the letter, I see that Fritz von Beckdorf threatens legal action. What an extraordinary thing to write to a stranger! So he wants to see the sword. I am half tempted to let him.

SEA VOICES

by Keith Miles

THE past is a ghost.

And Byron Morris, with his car roaring over coastal roads, sped into a future that was clamorous with promise. Experience, samples, jokes, toothpaste, attack. Byron knew how to pack for these trips. Surging between one life and the last, he exploited time to the full. His left hand fumbled, located, switched on, lifted the microphone. At seventy miles an hour, he poured words smoothly into the machine, like a barman pouring egg flip into a silver tankard. Replies, requests, acknowledgements, orders. At the end, separated from his business voice by a pause, then a lower octave, a personal and very personal message to Pat, his secretary. Pat would type up the letters. Plugged in behind a desk, Pat would listen to the ghost of Byron's voice and advance his business interests on an Adler Standard. Pat, like so many other Pats, would giggle and remember as she heard the recorded intimacy, which was meant for her and all the others alone.

The sea is a ghost. Those whispers are ghost stories.

Yet the wind did not disturb them. As it howled across the beach in search of new territory to terrorize, it had no effect on the two figures wearing anoraks on the rocks. The gulls cried above them and they offered up something to the gulls and all parties seemed happy with the transaction.

From his parked car and now strident radio, Byron Morris looked out to ignore the anoraks and to wonder about the girl. Was she working in this cold? Was she creating an out-of-season masterpiece? Crouched over her board, she laboured quietly. Occasionally, she looked up in the direction of the sea and listened. She was a young girl, eighteen maybe. She was a solitary girl. She was an accessible girl. Three reasons for making Byron Morris defy the whistle of the wind and leave his vehicle behind him.

Art is a ghost. It consorts with phantoms of the imagination.

'Painting, are you?'

The girl smiled at Byron. He corrected his mistake with grinning pedantry. 'Sketching, anyway. Used to be a dab hand with charcaol and pad myself.'

She smiled again. Nineteen, he decided. At most.

'Hardly need those sun-glasses this weather, my love. Hopeful eh?'

A third smile in succession. Yes, Byron. A potential Pat.

'On your own, then?'

Her nod triggered off his golden voice, his special Byronic voice, his dark and manly voice, his patter for this and every Pat. A few minutes of gold and her smile broadened into agreement. A probable Pat, Byron. Details. Now.

'The Ship. Eight. Always stay at the Ship.'

Why not, Byron? Attempt a metaphor, if you like.

'I've weighed anchor at the Ship many a time. Put port into every girl.'

Laughter from behind the sun-glasses.

'Interesting picture . . . can I see?'

Leave her, Byron. No need to stay. She's landed.

'But what's this figure on the beach . . . a body . . . man, woman? . . . I can't see any body. Are you drawing from Life or Mind?

Expressive dimples in her cheeks. She's quite Byronized.

'We'll talk about Mind tonight, my love . . . and bodies.'
Mutual laughter in the wind. A definitive Pat.

And all day long the voice of Byron rolled. He sold himself, his soul, his wares, his hope of salvation. Thrusting cases of samples before widening eyes, he demonstrated and assured, amused and impressed. Byron Morris on the make. Toy-selling was a toy in his hands. He filled windows with bendy rubber and whirring windmill. He loaded shelves with plastic cars and fragile dolls. He trinketed display stands and clogged up storerooms with buckets and spades and trumpets and This Is Something Entirely New. Participation, that was his secret.

'What about these masks? Dracula – Frankenstein's monster – the lot?'

He tried them on and achieved frightening verisimilitude.

'Novelty joke packs. A winner at any price.'

And he scattered itching powder on himself, or smoked a non-smoking cigarette, or drove a nail through his blood-soaked finger, or acquired a growth on his nose. Proprietors shook with merriment. When the season started in a few weeks, they knew they would be able to sell as easily as Byron sold. Byron conveyed such a feeling of confidence in a toy.

'And if you decide on anything else, Mr., Mrs., Miss, you can always get me, before closing time, at the Ship.'

The Ship is a ghost. Through the bottoms of its beer-glasses, you can see apparitions floating on froth.

'Have you heard the one about . . .?'

Strange. This ability of Byron's to clear a bar.

'Or there's the one about . . .'

Men, for the most part. Byron does not connect. They ease away.

'And one I must tell you . . .'

He makes the latest of late-nighters an early-bedder.

Byron cannot go on buying their drink and their attention indefinitely. Profit margins. Expense accounts. Commonsense. There are limits.

'Looking for someone, Mr. Morris?'

' "Byron" to you, my love.'

' "Mrs. Elias" to you, Mr. Morris.'

The licensee is emphatic. Byron has been Byron to her once, long ago. She heard the golden voice and went to his room that same night, no doubt to inquire about his comfort. Later, she returned to sleep in her own bed with the awakened ghost of the late Mr. Elias. Byron has widowed her familiarity. She will endure him as a customer once a year, but that, Mr. Morris, is all.

'Let you down, has she?'

'Not at all, not at all.'

Byron has looked at that watch every hour and still the girl from the beach has disappointed him. Seven, eight, nine, ten o'clock. Art students can tell the time, surely?

'Local girl, is she?'

Mrs. Elias presses home her advantage. Years too late.

'What's this, then? Someone lost?'

Sergeant Owen has called in for his habitual half and his annual spot of friction with Byron Morris, Sales Manager. Welsh Area.

'Can I be of any help, Mr. . . . um . . .'

'Morris!'

In the mouth of Mrs. Elias, the word sounds like a disease.

'What can I get you, Sergeant . . . Usual? Half, isn't it?'

And with that phenomenal memory and his reflex affability, Byron talks into a uniformed ear with zeal. He's not waiting for anybody, but he did notice somebody. On the beach. That morning. Girl, But the Sergeant must have. Couldn't miss her. Fair hair. Nineteen. Pretty? I'll say, boy! Name? Pat, or so I thought. Drawing all morning. A body washed up on the shore, Pat wore sun-glasses.

'We'll get *you* some sun-glasses, Mr. Morris!'

Law-enforcement humour. Heavy and functional as a cell door.

'And a white stick to go with it.'

Mrs. Elias sniggered her revenge after all these years.

'Seeing what isn't there, not seeing what is ... well, Mr. Morris, bach. Tell us this, then: Are you a blind man or a visionary? Is it Byron the Blind or Morris the Messiah?'

Two farmers, who had been conversing agriculturally in Welsh in order to exclude Byron, looked up as Sergeant Owen guffawed royally. He obligingly translated his joke into their native tongue and Byron was mocked anew. He made a ghost of the whisky in his glass and commissioned that a new life be born there.

'Well, must get back on duty ...'

Byron gave thanks inwardly.

'Hope we'll have no ... trouble from you this time, Mr. Morris. Eh?'

And with this warning reference to Byron's peccadilloes in the normally moral and law-abiding town, the Sergeant strode out.

'Yes, no trouble, Mr. Morris.'

Mrs. Elias underlined the warning, then withdrew to the other bar. Byron swallowed more alcohol and cursed silently. Trouble? From him? Never. What real trouble had he ever caused this small Welsh holiday resort? His behaviour that night had not been in the least scandalous. In any case, the policeman should not have shone the torch in there and then. Particularly there. The girl, named Pat, was over age. Byron had, once he found his clothes, been able to produce a licence. The car did have its lights on. Trouble? Anything but. Ask Pat.

Trouble is a ghost and it will always haunt you with its former acquaintance even when it is out of season.

'Would you care to join us?'

Byron looked up at the anorak. A woman, fortyish, English, lived inside.

'For a drink. My colleague and I have been most interested in what you've been saying throughout the evening.'

The word 'colleague' gave status to the other anorak. It, too, was woman. Older. Plainer. More intelligent.

'I'd love to. Look, what can I get you both?'

And waving aside the anoraked protests, Byron Morris responded to the glow of an audience once more. They both wanted him to talk. And talk. Friendship can defeat time. Temporarily. Years fell from the two ladies with each drink that Byron consumed. The colleagues had become his lifelong companions for the rest of the evening.

'And once, when I first went into selling – encyclopaedias, I think, no, wait, *medical* encyclopaedias – a woman invited me in to explain to her why I thought these expensive volumes, which I had never even opened, were the publishing event of the decade, as I had so persuasively described them.'

'What happened, Mr. Morris?'

'That would be telling!'

'Then tell us.'

So he did, and they smiled approvingly, shedding more years. They were both down to their twenties now. Neither of them were exactly up to the Pat standard, individually. But together, well, why not, Byron? Colleague Pats. Joint possibilities.

'Did you see her on the beach, the artist, the young girl?'

They had not, but then they had been too busy with their research and with the gulls above the rocks.

'What kind of research?'

'We're scientists, Mr. Morris. Of a kind.'

'We'll go into all that later, Mr. Morris.'

' "Byron," please.'

And they Byroned away to his heart's content. The older of the two scientific anoraks, who was now less than twenty-five, moved closer to him and pressed for clarification.

'Are you married or are you not?'

'Yes and no.'

They laughed dutifully and Byron explained.

'I do have a licence somewhere, and a wife somewhere else – God bless her – yes, and we even had a child. A girl, I think. Must be four, nine, twelve, by now. My wife and I parted, you see. That's to say, I can run faster than she can; and she's never caught me yet nor ever will.'

Mrs. Elias called for last orders and Byron stood his friends and himself a nightcap.

'Yes. Her name was Patricia. My wife.'

A wife is a ghost if you can see right through her, and if she walks out through the walls of a marriage.

'It's not far, Byron.'

How had he got into their van and what was all this equipment?

'Go on talking. We love your voice.'

Where was he driving between two teenagers in anoraks?

'Talk. We love your voice.'

'We know about voices.'

'Sound. That is what we research. Sound.'

'Scientists in sound.'

Had he talked for an hour before the van stopped?

'Here we are, Byron. Come on in.'

In which direction had they come and how would he return?

'Let's have a drink, shall we, Byron?'

No matter. The joint possibilities had matured as they had grown younger. Both were positives in the Pat sphere. Double Pats. A before and after Pat. A first then second Pat. A left and right Pat. A beneath and on top Pat. Yes, he would have another whisky, Pat.

The anoraks hanged themselves on hooks and the girls reclined on warm sofas. The cottage was large and well-appointed. Sound scientists did well, obviously. Perhaps there was something among all this gadgetry that could be adapted to Byron's purpose and palmed off on holiday children. Might he see this? How does that work? I bet those cost a bit, Byron. Ask more about these. Then, as he was about to divide and rule the Pats, as he was about come to terms with them, the offer.

'A thousand pounds!'

'In cash, Byron.'

'Here it is, Byron. See for yourself.'

He felt notes. Crisp, real, immediate.

'You want to give me one thousand pounds for my voice?'

'It's worth far more but that is all our Foundation allows us.'

'It's ridiculous ... all I have to do is to speak into the mike ...'

'And you're richer by one thousand pounds, Byron. Feel them again.'

'No need. You're on.'

And though the scientists in sound did look a trifle older and did put on dark spectacles for the recording, Byron was not dismayed. Technical fun beforehand would only heighten his desire. There were still two consecutive Pats waiting. Not to mention a thousand pounds by way of an honorarium. But first you must drink to silence, Byron.

'What is it, girls?'

'It will help to clear your throat. For the recording.'

How much had the gulls been paid for their voices?

Into his mouth Byron poured the liquid. It was sharp, cleansing. His mouth felt bigger. Examine that mouth, Byron. Take a mirror and study the ghosts around those lips. The shades of spent words, of betrayals, of boasts, of marital vows, of midnight promises. Spectres of kisses for this Pat or that. Drink, food, nicotine. A lot has come in and out of that mouth, Byron. A lot more will come in and out of it before this night is over. Yes, take the card. You can read.

'I, Byron Morris, do hereby give my voice for scientific purposes, in return for the payment of one thousand pounds.'

'Louder, please.'

Adjustments, earphones, amplifiers.

'I, Byron Morris . . .'

'With more urgency, please.'

'I, Byron . . .'

'Faster'

'I, B—'

'Faster still.'

'I—'

'All over.'

'All over, Byron.'

'There's your thousand pounds.'

A woman in her forties handed him the money. It was all there.

'Thank you, Byron.'

'You've been an immense help.'

'One can only do so much with gulls.'

'You have assisted our researches no end.'

They age with each second. Where have the two Pats gone?

'Goodbye, then, Byron.'

'Find your own way out.'

'And thank you again.'

'Did you want to say something, Byron?'

WAIT! Byron is mouthing madly. The loudmouth who is skilled in mouth-watering promises agitates his mouthpiece. It is as well that the two scientists can lip-read.

'Where is your voice?'

'On the tape of course. We own it now, Byron.'

'You sold it to us. Remember?'

It is not a joke, Byron. It is not one of your plastic gimmicks which you can thrust upon the juvenile population in order that it can irritate its elders. This toy works. This toy is real. This toy is not for sale, least of all at a thousand pounds. They will give you a demonstration if you will only stop thrusting the money into their faces. One of them, an anti-Pat, is depressing the switch.

'What the hell have you done with my voice?'

'Bought it, Byron.'

'Stop playing games, will you?'

'It was a fair agreement, Byron.'

'Fair. You give me my voice back or I'll—' Click.

Poor old dumb Byron. Cut dead by a female finger. Silenced by science. Work it out if you can, Byron. Five yards away is a machine and your voice. You here, it there. Thoughts within you, means of expressing them without. It is no use looking menacing. They have legal arguments. A finger presses another switch.

'I, Byron Morris, do hereby give my voice . . .'

Out of your own mouth you have been condemned. And you repeat your bargain louder, with more urgency, faster, faster still.

'I shouldn't do that, Mr. Morris.'

Mistake, Byron. To try and grab the machine.

'Goodnight, Mr. Morris.'

Down-graded to 'Mr. Morris' now. Morris the Mute. 'This is loaded.'

Two scientists with a real gun. Are they really kicking him out?

Night is a ghost. It haunts nightly.

Steal their van, Byron. Drive madly in all directions. Obey the pointing of all these fingerposts that flash by. You must get to town soon. But what then? How will you explain your predicament? Write it down. Of course. And what about your voice? Consult the gulls. Have they, too, been cheated by science of their means of speech? You must have a voice to voice your complaints, Byron. And you do! On your own tape-recorder back at the Ship. Find the town. Find the Ship. One of these fingers must point aright. There – lights, shapes, sea. Defy speed-limits, man. This is a matter of life and the death of a voice.

'Don't knock the door down!'

Nothing amiss with the voice of Mrs. Elias.

'I'm coming, I'm coming!'

And a dozen oaths confirm that her vocal abilities are intact.

'What are you trying to say, man!'

But Byron had lost patience with the former Pat and pushed past her to rush up to his room. There, he stops, transfixed. A picture on the wall is lit by the beam from a street-lamp. A picture that was not there before. A picture of the beach and the sea and a body which is clearly a man's. The girl's picture. Completed. She did exist. She did call at the Ship, after all.

'Come as soon as you can, Sergeant. Gone berserk, he has.'

Down below, Mrs. Elias plays the traitor. No time to reason with night-duty Sergeants. Grab your tape-recorder and go. Run, Byron. Make for the van. Drive, off you go, drive. You've got more power under your bonnet than the police car. You'll soon shake it off.

Forks and twists and bends in the road help Byron to shake off his pursuers long enough for him to switch on the tape-recorder. He will draw comfort from his own voice. He will be reassured by his own requests and replies and vocal nudges to Pat. Switch on.

'I, Byron Morris, do hereby give my voice . . .'

You should not have thrown it out of the van like that, Byron. It will not be covered by your expenses. The firm is particular about the safety of its equipment.

A light ahead. A farmhouse. No, *the* farmhouse. The one

that houses two anoraks and a stolen voice! Stop the van, creep up, look through the window. Over strong coffee, the scientists chat about sound and consider the day's takings. Don't rush, Byron. The tape recorder is there for the taking, but do not forget the gun. That stick will be ideal. Quietly. In you go. The door is on the latch.

'Mr. Morris. What do you want?'

'I thought we told you to . . . aw!'

The gun smashed from her hand by the weight of the stick.

'Leave that alone. It cost thousands.'

So did your voice, Byron. One thousand, anyway. Take the machine.

'Take your hands off it, or . . . ugh.'

Women have to be struck sometimes. Knock the other one out, too. They look better in repose. Now take the machine and go.

'Go round the back, Jones. And be careful. He may be dangerous.'

The law approaches.

'Hurry, Jones. He must be inside.'

Sergeant Owen is no court of appeal, Byron. You need time and apartness. Face a policeman with the theft of a car, breaking and entering, grievous bodily harm, a stolen machine, a lost voice and a previous warning for causing trouble and where will it get you? Find the back door and get away, even if the machine is heavy.

'This way, Sarge! He's making a run for it!'

'Come here, Jones.'

'But, Sarge.'

'These women need attention. Quick, man!'

Policemen turn nurses, then speak into transmitters.

Alone in a ditch, Byron Morris stops long enough to appreciate that the machine, true to the money expended upon it, operates on battery or mains. He flicks the switch marked 'battery', then presses another. Gulls call endlessly. He stops their sound, tries another switch.

'I, Byron Morris . . .'

Again, he kills the sound. A third switch.

'What on earth are you going to do, Byron?'

Himself. His own voice, strangered but loyal.

'Think. How are you going to get out of this one?'

He could go to the police.

'With all they've got on you? That Sergeant would think this was another of your jokes.'

Back home. Back to the office. Back to Pat.

'What use are you to any of them without me?'

The dialogue between two old friends is interrupted by whistle and dog. Where have all these men and animals come from? The police station in the town only runs to a few constables. Why the reinforcements? It is almost like a murder hunt.

'You did belt that woman hard.'

There was no blood, replies Byron.

'None visible you mean. Hey, come on, let's get out of here.'

Barking encircles and Byron lugs the machine down the ditch. His voice gets heavier at every step, but it is a burden he must carry. The dark is lightening into morning so he must make cover soon. A noise, a restlessness. He must be near the sea. He must have worked his way back to the shore. Rocks have pools. Water bears no scent.

Byron runs and strains and zig-zags and breathes violently though without noise. He wades through water and climbs over rocks. He ignores cuts and bruises and takes risks over crevices. At last, a hiding place. Safety. Dogs will never sniff him here in the salt air. High tide will never wash him out of this lair. The gulls who circle above cannot alert his pursuers because they have wings but no voice. You have made it, Byron. You are free. They will look in vain.

'Here. I'm over here!'

'That way, Sergeant!'
'Here I am! Come and get me.'
Why is the machine yelling at the top of its voice? Why is Byron unable to check the treachery of his own voice?
'Over here! Come on!'
'Follow me, men.'
'I'm waiting, Byron Morris is waiting.'
Try that switch, no, that, well pull out the batteries.
'I, Byron Morris, do hereby give notice . . .'
And with a long scream the voice and its undertaking are thrown far and deep into the sea. Byron has abandoned his voice. He has murdered his sound. But a voice is a ghost, too.

A voice is a ghost with a voice. From beneath the waves it calls to Byron with the golden harmony of a Byronic voice. It whispers in his ears the intimate messages which only he can whisper. It weakens, it convinces, it compels. With shivering policemen approaching over the rocks, a man stands up and yells at them with the voice of a hundred gulls then hurls himself into the sea. The manner of his fall from the high promontory suggests that he is searching for something down there, but we shall never know if he found it or not.

When the body was washed up two days later, it proved awkward under questioning. The Sergeant adjourned to the Ship.

'I've never seen that picture before, Mrs. Elias.'
Beach, sea, drowned man. As before.
'Had it for ages, Sergeant. Always meant to hang it in the bar.'
Look closer, Sergeant. The artist has signed the name of 'Pat', quietly, in the corner.

THE CONTRIBUTORS

F. TERRY NEWMAN was born in London in 1913 and derived his education from press-cuttings found in an eccentric aunt's attic during a childhood spent in Lincolnshire. He earns his living as a freelance journalist and is the editor of the *Spiritual Healer*; he is currently compiling a book of ghost stories of the Channel Islands.

PENELOPE FITZGERALD is the niece of the late Monsignor Ronald Knox, the mother of three children and the biographer of Edward Burne-Jones. She has seen two well-authenticated ghosts in Suffolk, but none since she and her family have moved to Clapham.

JOHN STEVENS was born in Lancashire in 1918, trained as an architect, and was elected to the R.I.B.A. in 1950. He now lives with his wife and three children in East Anglia, where his professional interests include teaching, writing and painting, and his non-professional interests include country-house gardens, prints and drawings, and mathematics.

FRANCIS KING was born in Switzerland in 1923 and spent his early childhood in India. Educated at Shrewsbury School and Balliol College, Oxford, he joined the British Council in 1949, serving in Italy, Greece, Egypt, Finland and Japan. He resigned from the Council in 1964 to devote himself entirely to writing. He is a past winner of the Somerset Maugham Award and the Katherine Mansfield Short Story Award, and is a Fellow of the Royal Society of Literature.

ELIZABETH LEFANU is better known as the composer

Elizabeth Machonchy. Her husband, William, is a great-nephew of J. S. Lefanu, the author of *Uncle Silas*. 'The Harpsichord' was written as a diversion for her elder daughter, Anna, her younger daughter, Nicola, is also a composer.

MICHAEL KERNAN is 48, was educated at Harvard and is married with three children. He has been a journalist for twenty-five years, during which time he has worked on newspapers in New York State, California and Washington, where for the last eight years he has been with the *Washington Post*. He has just returned to America after a year's sabbatical in London.

OLIVER KNOX is 51 and lives in Urbino, Italy. The first half of his life so far was spent at Eton and King's College, Cambridge, and in naval intelligence; the second half in advertising. Two years ago he sold his shares in his agency and started to write; his first novel, *An Italian Delusion*, appeared in the summer of 1975.

D. A. KOSTER was born in London in 1904, and is married with three sons. He joined the Merchant Navy in 1919, then in 1929 opened his own commercial art studio in London. He was commissioned into the R.A.F.V.R. in 1940, gained a permanent commission in the R.A.F. Marine Branch in 1950, and retired with the rank of Squadron Leader in 1958. The years 1959 to 1965 he spent on salvage vessels, as Second Mate, then First Mate, and finally as Master, as a result of which experience he published his first book, *Ocean Salvage*, in 1971. 'Nicola' is his first work of fiction.

SIR LAURENCE GRAFFTEY-SMITH was born in 1892 and educated at Repton and Pembroke College, Cambridge. He entered the Levant Consular Service of the Foreign Office in 1914, and retired in 1951 after four years as the first U.K. High Commissioner in Pakistan. Two books of memoirs, *Bright Levant* (1970) and *Hands to Play* (1975) record the assignments and vicissitudes of service which brought him the honours of K.B.E. and K.C.M.G. He is married, with two sons, and lives in Suffolk. His short stories and three radio plays have been broadcast by the B.B.C.

JULIAN BARNES trained as a linguist, a lawyer and a lexicographer, and abandoned each career successively. He is still, however, a young man, and no profession can afford to relax its guard. He writes regularly for the *New Statesman* and the *Times Literary Supplement*, and his first book, a literary history of Oxford, is due out in 1976.

PAUL THEROUX was born in Medford, Massachusetts, in 1941, and educated in the United States. He taught in Central and East Africa for five years and in Singapore for three, and has been living in London with his wife and two children since 1971. He has published eight works of fiction, the latest of which is *Sinning with Annie* (1975). A travel book, *The Great Railway Bazaar: By Train Through Asia*, has just been published.

BRIAN R. HALL is 41; he spent five years as a professional army officer, then fifteen years as a librarian, and has been writing full-time since 1974. His first children's book was published in 1964. He contributes regularly to a number of newspapers and periodicals. He is currently working on a five-volume fantasy based on the *Nibelungenlied*, and a three-volume fantasy for children.

KEITH MILES was born in 1940, and read history at Oxford. His first play was staged at the *Sunday Times* – N.U.S. Drama Festival. He became a freelance writer in 1967, since when he has had more than a dozen original plays broadcast on radio and television, together with many episodes of series, short stories and adaptations, as well as having four plays performed in the theatre. In the autumn of 1975 he published both his first novel and a critical study of the works of Günter Grass. He is married, with two children.

THE END

THE HAUNTING OF HILL HOUSE BY SHIRLEY JACKSON

There is so much horror in Hill House that nobody dares live in it. Only a ghost-hunting team would defy the spirits which haunt the house, and the one which gathers together to stay there for several weeks consists of four people. Their shocking experiences produce a real and ultimate terror culminating in a screaming climax which is as horrifying as it is unexpected.

THE HAUNTING OF HILL HOUSE is regarded by many as one of the most powerful horror tales ever told. It was filmed as THE HAUNTING. Shirley Jackson is also the author of the award-winning classic short story, THE LOTTERY.

0 552 10389 6 65p

STAR CHILD BY FRED MUSTARD STEWART

In a sleepy little Connecticut town, Helen Bradford had begun to have strange dreams. Sometimes they were wonderful dreams of a beautiful youth called Star Child who said he was coming from another galaxy to save mankind; but sometimes they were dreadful visions of something so horribly evil she couldn't even name it. At first the dreams came only at night, when she was asleep – and then they came during the day, when she was awake . . . they became stronger than reality . . . they *were* reality . . . And Helen found herself living a waking nightmare of insanity, where sex and violent death came to be one and the same thing . . .

0 552 10248 2 65p